SPECIAL FORCES CADETS

HIJACK

SPECIAL FORCES CADETS

CHRIS RYAN

⫘ SPECIAL FORCES CADETS ⫘
HIJACK

HOT
KEY
BOOKS

First published in Great Britain in 2020 by
HOT KEY BOOKS
80–81 Wimpole St, London W1G 9RE
Owned by Bonnier Books
Sveavägen 56, Stockholm, Sweden
www.hotkeybooks.com

A CIP catalogue record for this book is available from the British Library.

ISBN: 978-1-4714-0788-8
Also available as an ebook and in audio

1

This book is typeset using Atomik ePublisher
Printed and bound in Great Britain by Clays Ltd, Elcograf S.p.A.

Hot Key Books is an imprint of Bonnier Books UK
www.bonnierbooks.co.uk

SPECIAL FORCES CADETS

1

Night Terrors

It was dark and the wind was bone cold, but the whisky kept him warm.

Banfield staggered in a rough zigzag across the moor. The ground was marshy underfoot and the sodden grass bent and danced in various directions, battered by the gale coming in off the South Atlantic. Clouds scudded past a full moon. Now and then he stopped to look at them, but watching them made him dizzy. So he put the bottle to his lips, took another swig to settle his stomach and stumbled on.

Banfield's liking for the bottle was well known here on East Island. He and his wife owned a smallholding on the outskirts of Stanley, the capital of the Falkland Islands. Banfield was as tough and weathered as the sheep he farmed, but he still wore a heavy storm coat tonight. In conditions like this, he'd be mad not to.

Banfield might be a drunk, but he wasn't mad.

It was a lonely existence, farming sheep on the Falkland

Islands. The population was tiny and it sometimes felt as if the wider world barely knew they existed. Of course, once people across the globe had known the name of this tiny archipelago off the southern tip of Argentina. Nearly forty years ago, the Falklands had been a theatre of war between the British, who owned and occupied the islands, and the Argentines, who claimed them for their own. Banfield had been a teenager then, but he still remembered the fear and the fighting. In his dreams he relived the arc of tracer rounds across the landscape. The boom of artillery fire. He still saw the wounded soldiers, their skin burned. He would wake up sweating and trembling, his heart racing, and he would think the invasion was happening all over again. His wife would reassure him that he had been dreaming, but his anxiety remained long after he had woken up.

The only thing that eased his nightmares was the whisky.

His night-time wanderings had become a habit. Once he had a bellyful of whisky, his personality altered. He became angry, belligerent and – to his mind – brave. He would not be cowed by the memory of ghosts. He would burst out of the front door of his cottage, leaving it swinging in the wind, and march across the bleak, desolate moors that had once seen all that fighting. He would raise his arms to the sky, clutching the bottle, and scream defiance into the wind. But his voice was no match for the elements, and the only ears that heard him belonged to the incurious sheep. Nobody came here on the sunniest days, let alone in the middle of a gale and in the dead of night. The lack of an audience didn't stop him though. He would shout until his throat was raw, until the only thing to do was numb it with more whisky.

Tonight, he had shouted himself dry, though his face and beard were wet with the salt spray the gale had lashed through the night air. The ocean was a hundred metres away, and he was a good forty metres above sea level. Banfield realised he had instinctively walked the same route he had taken ever since he was a boy – to the top of a cliff overlooking an old smuggler's cove, facing east. As he battled towards it, the wind pushed him back. It screamed, banshee-like, in his ears, as if warning him not to go any further. Banfield didn't stop. Even when the wind knocked him down, he got to his feet again and carried on, clutching the bottle as if it was the hand of a child in danger.

He reached the top of the cliff. To his left were a collection of boulders and standing stones. As a boy, he used to hang out among those boulders with his friends, smoking cigarettes if they could find them. Now, though, he stood apart from them, a lone figure on the cliff edge. The moon disappeared behind the clouds. He collapsed onto the wet grass and stared out to sea. Banfield often thought that the ocean had a mind of its own. He had sat in this exact spot hundreds of times since he was a boy. Sometimes the sky had been blue and the air still. He had watched swifts and oystercatchers. After dark, he had occasionally seen nightjars, but tonight was too wild and windy for birds to be flying. He closed his eyes and briefly imagined the steely grey of naval ships on the horizon. That thought brought back the memory of his night terrors. He took another swig, his eyes still shut.

When he opened them again, the moon was out. His body

cast a faint shadow on the grass. He followed it with his eyes until he was looking over the cliff edge again, across the cove and out to sea.

Which was when he saw them.

There were three at first, or so he thought – his vision was a little blurred. But no, he could definitely see three figures emerging from the stormy waters. The water first at shoulder height. Then waist height. Knee height. Then they were running onto the beach. Banfield felt a sickening thud of panic in his chest. He quickly lay down on his front so he couldn't be seen on the clifftop, then wormed his way closer to the edge.

The three figures seemed to be crouching. He couldn't tell from this distance whether they were facing out to sea or inland. Banfield kept still and held his breath. Then he saw more figures emerging from the sea. A line of five this time, evenly spaced. A precise military manoeuvre. The sight triggered his memories. He started to shake. As he buried his face in the wet grass, he saw again the soldiers who had been burned during the war. He was a child again, and he wanted to cry. Perhaps he *was* crying. He wasn't sure.

How long he lay like that, face-down in the grass, Banfield couldn't have said. When he finally lifted his head and looked back over the cliff edge, however, he saw nobody. The figures on the beach had gone.

He blinked heavily, trying to refocus. Maybe he just couldn't see them any more.

No. The cove was empty. The figures had gone.

Or maybe, he thought as he knelt, they had never been

there in the first place. The world was spinning, after all, and he had drunk a lot of whisky. The moon was reflected in the silver waves crashing onto the sand. But it illuminated nobody. He examined the bottle again, then upturned it and poured the remaining contents out over the grass.

He stood up with difficulty and, not in full control, staggered close to the cliff edge. Too close. He managed to pull himself back just in time. Hyperventilating at the thought of what would have happened had he fallen, he gave the cove one last, sweeping glance. It was still deserted. He turned his back on it and hurried inland.

His mind had been playing tricks on him, he decided. He had not seen people emerging from the sea. His brain had been showing him the things he feared, not the things that were really there. It was the alcohol. He was glad he had emptied out the last of the whisky. He really should stop drinking it, he thought, as he retraced his steps back home.

2

Hunter-Killer

Marcus was twelve and bored.

He had thought today would be fun. His mum and dad had said that they would see a whale. Marcus had seen lots of *pictures* of whales, of course, and he knew loads about them. He knew that they spouted air from their blowholes and that some of them could do a flip above the water, and this was called breaching. He knew that killer whales were actually a type of dolphin, and he was excited at the thought that he might see one today on their whale-watching trip.

But all he had actually seen was the cold, grey water of the South Atlantic. No blowholes, no killer whales, not even so much as a porpoise.

Yeah. Boring.

He was on the starboard side of the boat, clutching the railings and leaning over the side. He was daydreaming about a killer whale bursting through the surface of the water, its teeth bared. All the other whale-watchers were on the port side – his mum and dad and little sister. The two grizzled sailors in charge of the boat. Three couples with grey hair who were even older than his parents. And five teenagers – three boys, two girls – who didn't seem to have any adults in charge of them.

Marcus couldn't wait until *he* was a teenager like them. Then he could do cool things like go on holiday without Mum and Dad. He *definitely* wouldn't choose the Falkland Islands though. It had taken so long to get here. A plane and then a boat, and he hadn't even been allowed to bring his iPad. *We're coming on holiday to spend some time as a family, not to stare at a screen.*

And now, to top it all, there were no whales.

He leaned a little further out over the railings, staring at the steely swell of the ocean. It was quite rough. Mum had given them all seasickness tablets, and the boat owners had almost cancelled the voyage before deciding at the last minute that it would be safe. Marcus wondered why you could see your reflection in water when it was still, but not when it was rough. Maybe he *could* see his reflection in the water, if he just leaned out far enough . . .

As he was trying this, the boat keeled heavily to starboard. Marcus felt a sickening emptiness in his stomach – not just because of the movement of the vessel, but because he realised he had been leaning out too far. He tried to grip the railings, but it was too late. He felt his feet leaving the deck, and saw the water coming terrifyingly close.

He was falling overboard . . .

Suddenly, he felt somebody grab his collar and pull him

back. His feet touched the deck again. The ship straightened. Marcus gasped in panic. He knew how close he had been to disaster.

'You okay, buddy?'

Marcus nodded, and turned to the person who had just saved him. It was one of the five teenagers. He had short brown hair, slightly messy from the sea breeze, thick eyebrows and a serious face.

'I'm fine,' Marcus said. He shrugged, as if to suggest he hadn't needed this boy's help at all.

'What's your name?'

'Marcus.'

'I'm Max,' said the boy. 'Hey, how about we go and join the others? They're telling us some pretty interesting stuff, you know.'

Marcus frowned. 'I bet you haven't seen any whales.'

Max smiled. 'No,' he said. 'No whales. But they're not the only things hiding under the water. C'mon, let's go find your mum and dad.'

'How come,' Marcus said as they walked along the deck towards the stern, 'you and your friends aren't with *your* mums and dads?'

Was it Marcus's imagination, or did Max's cheek twitch slightly?

'I guess we're just a bit older,' Max said.

'I'll be thirteen next year. Maybe then I'll be allowed to go on holiday by myself.'

'Yeah,' Max said with another smile. 'Maybe.'

They found the others standing in a group at the bow.

Marcus could tell that his mum and dad hadn't even noticed his absence. He hoped his new friend Max wouldn't tell them what had happened. As Max re-joined the other teenagers, Marcus hung around, hoping to make friends with them. They looked interesting. One of the boys was black, with tight dreadlocks and an unfriendly expression. He was chewing gum. The other boy was wiry and smaller, with a pleasant smile. He reminded Marcus of a kid at his school whose family came from Syria, and he wondered if that was where this lad came from. Of the two girls, one looked Chinese. She had long straight hair that blew wildly in the breeze, and she seemed to be scanning the horizon intently. The other was white: pale skin, blue eyes, thick brown hair and an intricate piercing in her left ear.

'Hey, everyone,' Max said. 'This is Marcus. Marcus, these are Lukas, Sami, Lili and Abby.'

The teenagers gave Max a funny look, as if to say, why are you introducing us to this kid? All of a sudden, Marcus understood. Max obviously thought he needed taking care of. He blushed, but he didn't say anything. The teenagers were cool. It would be more fun hanging out with them than with his mum and dad or – even worse – getting cornered by one of the old couples.

Abby pulled a bag of sweets from her waterproof coat and offered him one. 'Hey, Marcus,' she said. 'Bit of a bummer, hey? No killer whales and all.' She had an Irish accent.

Marcus hesitated. Jelly babies. Abby cocked her head. 'You like jelly babies, don't you?' She looked around conspiratorially and took a step closer. 'If you don't like jelly babies, you and me can never be friends.'

Marcus took a black jelly baby and popped it in his mouth. 'Thanks,' he said. He was about to tell Abby that the black ones were his favourites when one of the boat guys started talking.

If Marcus had been told to draw a picture of a sailor, he would have drawn someone like this. He had a weathered face and a grey beard and wore a yellow storm coat with a heavy hood. His voice carried over the sound of the wind and the sea.

'Right, everyone,' he said. 'I'm sorry the marine life is being shy today, but I've brought you to this patch of water for a good reason. Now, to land-lubbers like yourselves, one patch of sea probably looks very much like another. But to us sailors, every patch is different.' He seemed to gather his thoughts for a moment. 'In 1982, Argentina invaded the Falkland Islands. The British response was swift. Part of that response was to establish a total exclusion zone around the islands. Any Argentine warship or aircraft entering this zone would be liable to immediate attack by the British. On 30 April that year, a British nuclear-powered hunter-killer submarine, *Conqueror*, detected the Argentine warship ARA *General Belgrano* approaching the exclusion zone from the south-west. The following day, British intelligence intercepted an Argentine order to launch a massive attack on the British task force surrounding the islands. The *Belgrano* was to be part of that attack, and so the order was given by the Prime Minister of the day,

Margaret Thatcher, to sink it, even though it had not quite entered the exclusion zone.'

Marcus wasn't bored any more. Like the teenagers, he stared at the sailor, rapt.

'On 2 May 1982, the hunter-killer submarine fired three torpedoes at the *Belgrano*. Each torpedo was armed with an 805-pound Torpex warhead. Two of them hit the ship. The first blew off the ship's bow but was prevented from causing more damage by the internal torpedo bulkhead. It was the second torpedo that did the real damage. It punctured the side of the ship and exploded in the machine room. The explosion tore a twenty-metre hole in the main deck. Smoke filled the ship. Water gushed in through the hole. The electrics failed so there was no way to pump out the water or make a distress call. The *Belgrano* started to sink, and the captain gave the order to abandon ship. Argentine and Chilean ships came to the rescue and managed to save over seven hundred souls. But the attack killed three hundred and twenty-three, all of them consigned to a watery grave.'

There was a short silence, during which Marcus's head was full of thoughts of torpedoes and explosions and the deadly panic the men must have felt on board a burning, sinking ship. He put up his hand. 'Is this where the *Belgrano* sank?' he said.

The sailor shook his head. 'No, lad. The exclusion zone had a radius of two hundred nautical miles, much too far for a day trip like ours. But this area is where the British task force would have come under attack, had the *Belgrano* remained intact. And who knows how many men and women would have lost their lives then? We're sailing in the waters of a battle that never happened. I think that's a humbling thought.'

As the captain said this, Marcus watched the teenagers. It seemed very strange to him, but they all wore precisely the same expression. A furrowed brow. Narrowed eyes. Like his mum, when she was saying something that she *really* meant.

'I've lived on the Falkland Islands all my life,' said the sailor. 'We all live with the risk that we might come under attack again. Argentina is only three hundred miles away, and it still claims these islands are theirs. Who knows when they might have another go at reclaiming them?'

'If they do,' said Abby, 'we'll just have to fight them off again.'

For some reason, the adults on deck found that very funny. Marcus thought he understood why. It sounded like Abby was suggesting that she and her friends would be a match for the entire Argentine Navy. The adults laughed, but the teenagers didn't. They were taking what Abby had said deadly seriously.

The adults' laughter died away. There was an awkward silence. The five teenagers stared out to sea. Marcus stepped away from them and went to stand with his mum and dad. All of a sudden he didn't feel entirely comfortable in the presence of Max, Lukas, Lili, Abby and Sami. There was something about them. Something dangerous.

'Look! Marcus, look!' His mum was pointing out to sea. The grey arch of a whale had risen to the surface. Everyone gasped, and one of the teenagers laughed with surprise and pleasure. Marcus gripped the railings tightly again, his mum's hand fondly on his shoulder. All thoughts of war and battleships and dead sailors sinking to the bottom of the South Atlantic left his mind. They'd seen what they'd come to see, and Marcus wasn't bored any more.

3

Fish and Chips

The sun was setting as the whale-watching boat returned to harbour. Max fist-bumped the kid he'd prevented from going overboard. 'Take it easy, Marcus,' he said.

Marcus nodded. Ever since the ship's captain had told them about the Falklands War and the *Belgrano*, he'd seemed shy of Max and his friends, Max thought. It was obvious that Marcus had understood on some level that they weren't quite who they said they were. The adults on the boat, of course, had paid them no attention. Sometimes, youngsters could be far more perceptive than grown-ups.

Which was why the Special Forces Cadets existed in the first place.

Max, Lukas, Abby, Lili and Sami made a special effort to thank the ship's crew for the whale-watching tour as they disembarked. It wasn't just that they wanted to be polite. Today's trip was part of their cover. They wanted their presence to be remembered, maybe even commented upon. Perhaps tonight, over a pint in the pub, the skipper would mention that he'd had five teenagers on his boat. The more people were aware of them doing ordinary tourist activities, the more easily they would accept that they *were* ordinary tourists.

Which they were not.

It was a short walk from the harbour at Stanley, the capital of the Falkland Islands, to the guest house where they were staying. In the forty-eight hours since they had arrived on a military aircraft from RAF Brize Norton, the airbase in Oxfordshire, the cadets had taken pains to ensure that they were seen around the town. They had soon become familiar with the geography of this small, quaint capital. Here, thousands of miles from home, they had been surprised to find British supermarkets and cosy pubs. There were red telephone boxes and union flags flying from several houses. It felt to Max like a tiny seaside resort.

'Fish and chips?' he suggested as they approached one of the main streets.

'What?' said Lukas, Sami and Lili in unison. Max had forgotten that, as they came from America, Syria and China respectively, fish and chips weren't really on their radar.

'You haven't lived,' Abby said, 'till you've had fish and chips.' She led them into the shop where a red-faced man stood behind the counter. 'Cod and chips, five times,' she said.

The man nodded and started scooping chips from the fryer. 'Been out on the boat, have you?' he said.

That was good, Max thought. It meant he knew who they were, and had accepted their cover story.

'Yep. Birdwatching tomorrow,' Abby said. 'Up on the moors. We're hoping to see some penguins while we're here as well. Er, do you think I could have a gherkin too?'

'One gherkin coming up.'

'And a pickled egg.' She turned to the others and saw their faces. 'What?' she said. 'I'm hungry!'

Outside the chip shop, the cadets sat on a low stone wall and unwrapped their parcels of food. 'Eat up,' Max said quietly. 'It's going to be a long night.'

'A cold one too,' Lili said, 'by the feel of it.' And it was true. The temperature had suddenly dropped and there was a biting wind.

'I wouldn't mind being Woody and Angel right now,' Abby said. 'Comfortable bed, nice warm ship.' She nodded out to sea as she popped a chip into her mouth. Woody and Angel were the cadets' Watchers: the adults who, along with their leader Hector, had selected and trained them and who were currently stationed on a British naval patrol vessel in the waters surrounding the islands. With a bit of luck, that's where they would stay.

But luck, the cadets had been taught, was not something to be relied upon. Sharp skills and a clear head were likely to keep you alive longer.

'Do you really think having Woody and Angel here would make people suspect us?' Lukas said, frowning.

'Not exactly,' Max said. 'But the five of us being here by ourselves means that any Argentine spies in the vicinity

16

are going to actively discount us if they're searching for anybody suspicious. And it could be anyone. The captain of that ship we were on today. The chip guy.'

'Hope it's not the chip guy,' Abby said, her mouth full. 'I liked him. He pickles a mean egg.'

'What I mean is,' said Max, 'we can't trust anyone. We need to make sure that everybody we meet thinks we're just here for the wildlife.'

'Good job we've got Max to remind us of this stuff, hey, guys?' Abby said.

Max gave a rueful smile. Maybe he *had* been a little patronising. But it did no harm to remind themselves of why they were here, even if the Watchers had briefed them all thoroughly about the curious rumour that had reached British intelligence just under a week ago . . .

It had started, by all accounts, with an old farmer called Banfield. The cadets had seen a photo of him. His face looked pinched by the weather and reddened by his fondness for the bottle. He had bumped into the governor of the Falkland Islands late one evening, plainly the worse for wear. Slurring his words, and with one arm around the governor's shoulder, he said that he'd seen figures emerging from the sea into a secluded cove late the previous night. The governor hadn't taken him seriously. The farmer had a reputation as a drunk and he couldn't sensibly answer any of the governor's follow-up questions.

— *How many figures did you see?*

— *Five,* said Banfield. *No . . . fifteen . . . no . . .*

— Did they reach the shore by boat?

— No, no, there were no boats. No boats at all.

— What did these figures do after they came ashore?

— Ah, that's the strange thing, said Banfield. *They completely disappeared.*

— Had you, by any chance, had a drink?

— Absolutely not! Well, maybe a little something to keep the cold at bay, Governor . . .

The governor had reported the conversation back to London. Two days later, Hector was briefing the cadets in his usual surly, no-nonsense style.

'There has been intelligence chatter in the South Atlantic for several months now,' he told them as they sat in the first-floor briefing room at Valley House, their home and headquarters in the wilds of Scotland. 'Argentina is showing a renewed interest in the Falkland Islands. But there's been no direct evidence of a second attack.'

'Until now,' Lili had said.

'Maybe. The uncorroborated word of a drunk sheep farmer is hardly convincing. We can't trust him. There's no way the British government would make accusations against Argentina, or deploy a task force to the region, on such a flimsy pretext. At the same time, we can't ignore this information completely. We need independent verification that this farmer really saw what he thinks he saw.'

'Let me guess,' said Lukas. 'That's where we come in?'

'Right,' Hector said. 'Ordinarily we would deploy an SAS team to put in surveillance on the island. But there's a problem. We've reliable intelligence that the Argentines have agents embedded in the Falklands. We're fairly sure they have regular islanders on their payroll, probably living in Stanley. But there's also some evidence to suggest that there's a mole at the local RAF base at Mount Pleasant. We can't guarantee that an SAS deployment to the Falklands would remain a secret.'

'Why does it need to remain a secret?' Max asked. 'The Falklands are British, aren't they? Surely we can send whoever we want there.'

'True,' Hector said. 'But if we arouse the Argentines' suspicion, they may well change their tactics. Sometimes, the best course of action is to let the enemy continue, unaware that you know what they're doing. That way, you can make an informed decision about how best to stop them. The Falklands has a tiny population and newcomers are easily noticed. But if five teenagers turn up on, say, a wildlife-watching holiday, not even the most suspicious Argentine agent is going to think they're there to put in military surveillance.'

'One of these days,' Abby said, 'you'll let us go on a *real* holiday.'

'You think?' Hector said.

'Not really.'

'Good. For a minute there, I thought you were going soft on me. There's a weekly RAF flight to the Falklands. It also transports civilians. It leaves Brize Norton at midday tomorrow. You'll be on it. When you arrive in Stanley you'll check in to the Atlantic View guest house in the centre of town. Woody and Angel will be stationed on a Royal

Navy patrol ship that regularly sails the waters around the Falklands. They'll have a Special Boat Service unit with them – they're like the SAS, but on water. Ostensibly they'll be on exercises, which is perfectly normal. But if you get into trouble, or you need backup, they'll be there. Meanwhile, by day you'll be straightforward nature tourists: whale-watching, birdwatching, rambling – you get the picture. By night, you're to put in covert surveillance on the cove where this farmer claims to have seen the figures coming ashore. If there's a repeat performance, you're to find out what their objective is.'

'What do you *think* their objective is?' Lili asked.

Hector glanced uncomfortably at Woody and Angel, who were standing at the far end of the room. 'If pushed,' he said, 'I'd say that we're dealing with Argentine special forces scoping out possible landing sights and making advance preparations for an invasion. If – when – it happens, such an invasion will be swift and well planned.' His eyes narrowed. 'You're too young to remember the Falklands War,' he said. 'But I'm not. My own father was part of the task force, and he told me some grisly stories about men dying badly. We have the opportunity to ensure that doesn't happen again. This might sound like a straightforward surveillance operation, but there's a hell of a lot riding on it. Don't let me down.'

Don't let me down. Hector's voice rang in Max's ears as he sat with his friends. The skipper's description of the sinking of the *Belgrano* had spooked him a little. He felt weighed down by the responsibility to ensure that this mission went well. The cadets had found themselves in some scary situations before, but they'd never had to avert a full-blown war. He couldn't help wondering how many people would die if they failed.

He became aware of Sami, who was sitting next to him. His Syrian friend was holding up a fat, half-eaten chip, smeared in salt, vinegar and ketchup. His eyes were wide.

'What?' Max said.

Sami turned to him. 'I thought you were my friend,' he said.

Max frowned. 'I . . . I am.' He felt genuinely upset at the thought that Sami might think anything else.

'Then why did you never tell me about fish and chips before?' He looked back at his half-eaten chip. 'That is the most delicious thing I have ever eaten,' he said, before cramming the rest of the morsel into his mouth. 'I can't believe I had to come all the way to the Falkland Islands to try it!'

4

Atlantic View

The Atlantic View guest house was a simple place. The cadets each had a single room with a lumpy mattress and, as the name suggested, a vista across the ocean, obscured by thin net curtains. The guest house was on the outskirts of Stanley and the cadets were the only guests. It was run by an old woman called Arlene who was proud of her enormous breakfasts. When she wasn't cooking bacon, she seemed to spend her time in front of the television in a tiny front room with a log burner. When the cadets returned home that evening, there she was, a cup of tea on the occasional table by her armchair. They wouldn't see her for the rest of the evening.

They retired separately to their rooms. Max checked the time: 1930 hours. It was dusk. He parted the net curtains and looked out over the Atlantic. A low moon was reflected on the water, disappearing now and then as clouds scudded across it. They would not be able to rely on moonlight tonight.

Fortunately, that didn't matter.

Max's suitcase was under his bed. He pulled it out and plonked it on top of the mattress, which squeaked under the weight. The main compartment of the suitcase was empty, but there was a second, hidden, compartment underneath, which he unzipped. Here, there was an encrypted satellite phone; a pair of high-resolution night-vision binoculars, with extra battery packs; and a small digital camera with a telescopic lens. Max took the binoculars and turned off the lights in the room. He switched on the binoculars and put them to his eyes. The contents of the room appeared, massively blurred: he could kind of make out the shapes of the bed, the rickety writing table, the tea-making tray with its little packets of biscuits, but only with difficulty at such close range. The NV was working though, and that was the main thing. He went over to the window and parted the net curtain again. He saw a Land Rover moving along the harbour road, and a cat curled up on the roof of an outhouse. A few people hurried along the sea front, wrapped up against the breeze. And there was a ship, very distant, out at sea.

Satisfied that the binoculars were in full working order, Max switched them off and turned the lights on again. There was a knock on the door. 'Yeah?'

It was Sami. 'Have you checked your optics?' he said.

'Just now. What is it, mate? You seem worried.'

Sami shrugged and walked over to the window. 'It's going to be a dark night,' he said.

'Dark nights are good,' Max said. 'We won't be seen.'

23

'I guess.'

'What is it, Sami?'

Sami turned. 'Do you ever get the feeling that we're the wrong people for this job?'

Max sat on the edge of his bed. 'Sometimes,' he said. 'They call it imposter syndrome, don't they?'

'Do they? I just . . . from what I've heard, a lot of people died in the Falklands War, on both sides. It feels like a big deal, leaving it up to us to stop it happening again.'

'I guess,' Max said. 'But really it's up to other people not to start it, right? Soldiers don't start wars. We just do what we're told, and we try not to make too many mistakes along the way. I bet that's what Hector would say, anyway.'

'I suppose so,' Sami said. 'It's so quiet here – on the islands, I mean. It feels like – what's the phrase? – the calm before the storm.' He headed towards the door. 'We leave at 2300 hours, right?'

'Roger that,' Max said. 'Hey, Sami.'

Sami stopped and turned.

'We've done okay so far. Four missions down and we're all still alive and pretty much in one piece.'

Sami nodded, but he still looked uncomfortable. 'I'll see you later,' he said.

Once Sami had left, Max lay on his bed. It was important that Arlene thought they had all retired for the night, because then she would go to bed and they could sneak out unnoticed. He tried to rest – they had a long night ahead of them – but couldn't. Truth was, he shared Sami's worries.

The hours passed in silence, broken only by the creaking of the old guest house. At half past ten, Max stood up and started to get ready. He had unpacked his clothes into an old wooden wardrobe, and now he selected the gear he wanted for tonight's surveillance operation. It would be cold and possibly wet. He put on three T-shirts so the layering effect would keep him well insulated. Black waterproof trousers. Breathable woollen socks and sturdy Gore-Tex walking boots. A breathable storm coat. He remembered, back in the children's home where he had been brought up, reading a book by the old fell-walker Alfred Wainwright. What had he said? *There's no such thing as bad weather, only unsuitable clothing*. Back then, Max never dared to imagine that one day he would be choosing clothing for a situation like this.

He packed his NV binoculars and digital camera in his storm-coat pockets and, almost as an afterthought, put his pillows under his blankets to give the impression that someone was sleeping there. At 11 p.m. precisely he exited the room, switching off the light and turning the key in the lock behind him. The others were waiting in the corridor. Nobody spoke. They crept one by one down the stairs, making as little noise as possible. On the ground floor, Lili used the key Arlene had given them to open the front door. They exited quietly and locked the door behind them.

It had started to rain. Not heavily, but enough to ensure that the street in front of the guest house was deserted. The cadets headed west, past weather-boarded houses that were closed up for the night. Stanley was such a tiny town that they were beyond its boundary in less than five minutes. A straight road headed along the coast, following the line of the inlet on which the town was situated. The cadets kept a few metres to the left of the road, ready to hit the grass if a vehicle came in either direction. But none did. As the lights of Stanley receded behind them, Max felt an increasing sense of solitude.

The rain became stronger. It whipped against their faces, and stung. They reached the end of the coastal inlet. Here, both the shoreline and the road turned back in a hairpin. Now the cadets struck off to the north. This direction took them across country, away from the road. Max knew that from here it was about five hundred metres to their destination.

The steepness of the hill gradually increased, and so did the ferocity of the elements. A strong wind blew directly into their faces, and the cold rain pelted them. But although they were thousands of miles from Valley House, these bitter conditions were entirely familiar to them. They had trained in weather like this and hiked for many miles in the darkness. There was a strange comfort in knowing that they had done this before. Max noticed that the steeper the hill and the worse the weather, the faster they moved. Within a couple of minutes, they were jogging uphill, powering through the elements. The exercise and the layers he wore kept Max warm and, although he sweated, his pulse was low and his breathing even. The Watchers' high-intensity fitness regime was obviously working.

It was five minutes past midnight when they reached the top of the hill. Lukas, who was leading, held up one hand. The cadets came to a halt. If Max's internal compass and detailed study of a map of the islands were correct, they were approaching their destination: the clifftop overlooking the cove where the old farmer, Banfield, claimed to have seen men coming out of the sea.

Wordlessly, the cadets hit the ground and advanced on all fours. Otherwise, as soon as they reached the clifftop, their silhouettes would be visible from the cove. So they kept low, the wet grass brushing their faces, the rain falling heavily on their backs. Ten metres. Twenty metres.

'Don't you just love Hector's little holidays?' Abby whispered as they approached the edge of the cliff.

They stopped just before the edge and looked down.

It was a good job none of them suffered from vertigo. The drop down to the beach was sheer, and they were at least forty metres high. Max removed his NV binoculars from his storm coat. The others did the same. Together, they scanned the shoreline below.

It was a sandy beach. If this really had been a holiday, and it wasn't the middle of the night, and it wasn't raining, the cove would be a lovely place to go. Tonight, though, battered by the elements, it was unwelcoming. The waves crashed heavily against the shore and the high cliff was dark and imposing. At the eastern side of the cove was a winding ridge that led up to the top of the cliff. Max estimated that it would take between five and ten minutes to ascend it, and half that time to make a descent. The wind shrieked overhead. It was that, more than the weather, that chilled Max. It occurred to him that, if an anxious brain were to invent a scary sight, this would be a place where it was likely to happen. But perhaps the farmer really had seen something . . . Looking out over the cove, Max suddenly wished he was anywhere but here.

He raised the binoculars. White foam from the breaking waves was blowing in the direction of the wind, which told him it was at least a force six or seven gale. There was no sign of any ships. No sign of anything but the bleak vista of the South Atlantic.

'Could be a long night,' Lukas muttered.

To Max's right, in the direction of the ridge, there was a hump in the terrain. About fifteen metres to his left was a group of large, misshapen boulders. They would offer some protection from the wind and would allow the cadets to stay hidden. At his suggestion, the cadets crawled towards the boulders and crouched on the leeward side, away from the cliff edge. Further along the cliff, about fifteen metres away, a ditch meandered inland, away from the cliff. Beyond that was a solitary copse of trees. For a moment Max wondered if the ditch would be a better place to set up their observation post. But although it was deep enough to keep them hidden, it was too exposed to the elements. Morale was an important factor in a decision like this: they would stay a little warmer and drier among the boulders.

'We'll take it in turns to keep watch over the cove,' Lili said. 'Whoever's not doing that should check the area behind us to make sure we're not discovered. I'm happy to go first.'

'I'll join you,' Sami offered. Together, they crawled away from the boulders, back towards the cliff. Max, Abby and Lukas took up surveillance positions where they were and scanned the ground behind them.

There was nothing to see. Empty moorland. Rain. No wildlife. No humans.

They remained in those surveillance positions for a full hour. Max's muscles started to ache from cold and lack of movement. The wind bit into his fingers as they held the binoculars. He thought longingly of his warm bed back at the guest house. Then he forced that thought from his mind, because it was compromising his ability to remain watchful. He could hear Hector reprimanding him. *If you can't take a night's surveillance in the wet, maybe you're just not tough enough for this job . . .* There had been a time when Max thought Hector's brutal pronouncements were over the top. Now he knew that his uncompromising attitude had kept the cadets alive, more than once . . .

He was glad when Lili returned to the boulders to say it was time to swap positions. He crawled with Abby and Lukas to the cliff edge, where Sami was still surveying the cove. Lying on his front, he raised his binoculars and was greeted by the now familiar sight of the beach.

'You think we're going to see anything at all tonight?' said Lukas, who was lying next to him.

Max didn't reply.

Not immediately.

Something had caught his eye.

Three figures had appeared in the water, several metres out. The sea, waist high at first, swelled up to their necks, then subsided. The figures waded forward.

'I already have,' Max said quietly. 'Look.'

5

Frogmen

Max, Lukas and Abby watched in silence.

The three figures made it to shore. His NV binoculars gave Max a clear view of them. They were frogmen: divers with masks and rebreathers. Neoprene wetsuits clung to their skin and they were carrying assault rifles, from which seawater gushed as they emerged. They ran onto the beach, fanned out and knelt down, their rifles raised. They covered the area as more frogmen appeared from the sea: two lines of five, some of them armed, some of them carrying heavy rucksacks.

'Whale-watchers?' Abby said quietly.

All the frogmen were on the beach now. Two of them, clearly the leaders, directed the others with hand gestures. The figures jogged away from the shoreline towards the cliff. In a matter of seconds, they were out of view. Max kept the binoculars on the water. Something didn't add up. There was no sign of any boats, but the frogmen were carrying too much gear to have swum far. How had they got here?

'What do we do now?' Abby asked.

Max thought for a moment. The first part of their objective was simple: to put in surveillance on the cove and attempt to verify the farmer's story. They had done that. Mission accomplished. The second part of their objective was more difficult: follow the intruders and find out what they were doing.

'I think there's only one exit from that cove,' he said. 'The ridge on the eastern side. We need to put in an observation post at the top of it. If they head up it, we can follow them. If not –'

'*Guys!*' It was Lili's voice, a harsh, urgent whisper. '*We've got a problem. Get over here . . .*'

Max, Abby and Lukas rolled back from the cliff edge and crawled over to the boulders. Sami was crouched to the side of one of them, binoculars to his eyes, scouting out the grassy terrain.

'What is it?' Abby asked.

'There's someone coming,' Sami whispered.

Max raised his binoculars. He saw the figure immediately. Approximate distance: a hundred metres.

'Is it one of the frogmen?' Lukas asked.

'I don't think so,' Max said.

'How do you know?' Abby demanded.

'He's not wearing the gear. Plus, he's kind of . . . zigzagging.' Max paused for a moment. 'Like he's drunk.'

'He's carrying a bottle,' Sami added. 'Can you see?'

Sami was right. Focusing on the figure's hand, Max could see it. 'You know who I think that is?'

The others replied in unison. 'The farmer.'

He was definitely coming their way. Although he was meandering, he was closing in on the cadets' position. If they stayed here at the boulders, there was a good chance he would find them. If they headed to the top of the ridge to avoid him, he would see them moving: there was a bump in the terrain that would make them instantly visible to him.

'We need to get to that ditch,' Max said, lowering his binoculars. 'These boulders are an obvious landmark for him to head to, for shelter.'

'What if he finds us?' Sami asked.

'Then we talk our way out of it. But if we stay here, we're more likely to be discovered. Does everyone agree?'

The cadets nodded.

They crawled to the ditch on all fours. It was about fifteen metres away and, on reaching it, they found that it was about a metre deep. It followed a slight gradient down to the cliff edge. A steady stream of water ran along it. The cadets knelt in the cold stream. The wind moaned along the ditch, making it colder here than it had been on the clifftop.

'We get all the best jobs,' Abby muttered as the cadets settled in to their new OP.

Somewhere, in a semi-sober corner of his mind, Banfield knew he shouldn't have come out again. He knew that the people he had told about the men at the cove hadn't believed him, and they laughed at him behind his back. And he knew he'd had even more to drink this evening.

But the semi-sober corner of his mind wasn't in control. He stopped, raised his half-empty bottle and roared in frustration. The wind was louder than his voice.

Up ahead, he saw the boulders on the cliff edge where he had spent so much time as a boy. Those dark shapes were like old friends and he felt an urge to be among them. He staggered towards them, only half aware of his inability to keep a straight line.

He stopped, took another swig from his bottle, and carried on.

Max peered over the edge of the ditch while the others kept their heads down.

He could see the farmer with his naked eye. Occasionally the old man stopped and raised his bottle to the sky before carrying on. More than once, Max thought the man would fall over. But he managed to stay upright, despite his stumbling gait.

Then Max saw movement elsewhere. His blood froze.

Three figures appeared beyond the boulders, at the top of the ridge leading from the cove to the clifftop. Very slowly, Max put his NV binoculars to his eyes and focused in on the figures. One look confirmed his suspicion. The men still wore their diving suits and had rucksacks on their backs. They carried assault rifles and wore night-vision goggles. Everything about them said special forces. They scanned the area, weapons raised. Max suddenly felt highly exposed, peering out over the edge of the ditch. Although this was the best hiding place they could find, it was not a good one. He ducked down into the ditch again. 'Don't move,' he hissed at the others. 'The frogmen are coming . . .'

Banfield's world was spinning. Ten metres short of the boulders, he fell to his knees. He had to shut his eyes to stop the nausea. He staggered to his feet again and stumbled onwards.

He reached the closest boulder and put his hand against the cold stone, steadying himself.

Then he saw them.

They were to his right. Three men in black. They had seen him and were approaching. They had weapons. And the weapons were pointed directly at Banfield.

Banfield stared at his bottle. Then back at the figures. He closed his eyes and shook his head. When he opened them again, the figures were still there. Only closer. Ten metres.

Banfield started shouting. 'What are you doing here? What are you . . . what are you doing here? Go back to where you came from! You don't . . . don't belong here . . .' His words were slurred, his sentences incomplete. A knot of anxiety burned in his chest, but he held up his bottle like a weapon, ignoring the whisky that sloshed down his arm and onto the wet grass. Then he staggered towards the gunmen, still shouting, his words once more drowned out by the wind.

But the wind carried his voice to the cadets' hiding place. *What are you doing? Go back! You don't belong here!*

'What's happening?' Lili hissed.

'It's the farmer,' Max said. 'I think he's challenging the frogmen.'

'But they're armed!' Lili said. 'They'll kill him. We have to do something!'

She started getting to her knees.

'*No!*' Max hissed, pulling her back down. 'Think about it. If they were going to shoot him, they'd have done that already.'

Lili froze. 'I don't know.'

'We don't have an option,' Max interrupted. 'They're armed, we're not. If we show ourselves . . .'

He thought she was going to argue. But she didn't. Instead, she manoeuvred herself so she could just see over the edge of the ditch. Max knew better than to try to dissuade her. Lili was determined. Reluctantly, he joined her.

'What the hell does he think he's doing?' Max breathed.

Banfield was roaring at the frogmen now, brandishing his bottle like a caveman's club. The three gunmen had surrounded him. Their weapons were raised, pointing at his chest, their barrels just out of reach of his bottle. He spun around, jabbing the bottle at them. It even clunked against the barrel of one of the rifles.

'Get away from here!' he shouted. '*Get away from here!*'

One of the gunmen lowered his weapon. Banfield felt a surge of triumph. They were listening to him at last.

His triumph was short-lived.

The gunman let his weapon hang across his chest. He wore goggles that obscured his eyes. Now he flipped them up. Banfield couldn't help gasping. There was something monstrous about his eyes. Even by the silver light of the moon, Banfield could tell that the whites of his eyes were not white at all, but so bloodshot that they appeared completely red. He gaped at them, then noticed other features: a black tattoo that crept up the man's neck and onto his left cheek. A double razor slit in his right eyebrow. They were clearly intended to make him appear threatening, and they did, but it was the eyes that were worst.

The gunman stepped forward and, with a grin and a violent swipe of his arm, knocked the bottle from Banfield's fist. In an instant he had one arm around the farmer's neck and had forced Banfield's arm up behind his back.

Banfield tried to shout again, but he couldn't: the pressure on his throat was too strong. He suddenly felt himself being pushed towards the cliff and began to struggle furiously. But the man with the red eyes was too strong. He forced Banfield across the wet grass, through the wind and the rain, until they were teetering at the very edge of the cliff.

'His eyes,' Lili whispered.

Max knew what she meant. The soldier's eyes were red, like fire, and for a dreadful moment Max thought he was looking right at him. But then he turned his back and pushed the old man to the edge of the cliff.

'No!' Lili whispered.

But even she could see that there was nothing they could do.

Max was frozen in horror next to her. In the ditch, Abby demanded an update. But neither of them answered. It was as if they were watching a horror movie in slow motion. They didn't want to watch, but they couldn't take their eyes off it.

Banfield didn't feel drunk any more. He felt stone-cold sober. His toes were over the cliff edge and the only thing that stopped him from falling was the man holding him from behind.

Fear flashed through him. The moon appeared from behind the clouds and suddenly illuminated the cove below. He could see the sand, and the waves crashing on the beach, and the jagged rocks immediately below. His assailant said something in the Argentine Spanish that Banfield had never bothered to learn, in a harsh, guttural voice. But he understood the man's tone, and he knew the end was coming.

He felt the arm around his neck loosening. He attempted to struggle one final time, twisting his body around in the vain hope that he could escape.

But of course he couldn't. All it took was a gentle push in the small of his back. His feet slipped over the edge. His arms, suddenly released, wheeled in the air as he tried to keep his balance.

They continued to spin as he fell from the cliff edge, and they only stopped when he slammed onto the beach below.

Max and Lili stared in horror. The farmer had screamed as he fell, but the scream had died away immediately, dissipating into the wind.

They had just witnessed a murder.

A dread chill closed around Max's heart. They had done nothing to help that man. Nothing at all. And it was his fault. He had stopped Lili from going to his aid.

'We . . . we couldn't have done anything,' Lili whispered. She took Max's hand and squeezed it in reassurance.

But there was no time for that. The man who had thrown the farmer off the cliff had re-joined the others.

The men raised their weapons again and started to walk towards the cadets.

6

Minisub

Max and Lili crouched with the others in the ditch, out of sight.

The rain had stopped but the wind was still strong. It blew the clouds fast across the night sky. As they slid past the moon, it caused a strange strobe effect. One moment, the cadets were lit up. The next, they were in shadow.

Max was shocked into silence. Even if he had wanted to tell the others what he'd just seen, he couldn't. The frogmen were approaching. Silence was essential: these men were killers. Max breathed deeply, trying to stay calm.

Not easy. The guilt he had felt when the red-eyed frogman had flung the farmer over the edge still pounded through him, no matter what Lili might have said to make him feel better.

Thirty seconds passed.

The voices, when they heard them, were much closer than Max expected. He could hear two men speaking in Spanish. One of them had an unusually guttural voice. He estimated that they were no more than five metres from the ditch. He held his breath, doing everything he could not to move or make a sound. The other cadets were statue-still, crouched next to him. The moon suddenly appeared from behind a cloud, so brightly that it cast a shadow of the nearby frogmen over the ditch. Max felt nauseous. If they came even a step closer, they would see the cadets . . .

The moon disappeared again. Darkness engulfed the cadets. A moment later, the frogmen spoke. Max could tell from the volume and direction of their voices that they were not so close as before. They had moved along the ditch, away from the cliff edge. A wave of relief crashed over him. He allowed himself to breathe.

'What's happening?' Sami whispered.

'They threw the farmer over the cliff,' Max whispered back. And because he knew Sami well, and understood how his friend loathed injustice, he gently held his forearm to keep him still. He calmed himself – and his guilt – with another deep breath. 'Remember, we need to find out who they are and what they're doing.'

'But –'

'They're armed, Sami,' Lukas cut in, in a harsh whisper. 'We're not. We can't fight them. Max is right. Stay still.'

Which they did. The rain returned, pelting down on their hunched backs. The wind blew fragments of conversation their way, but it was hard to tell who was speaking or how far away they were. The cadets remained like that for fifteen minutes, then Max and Lili gingerly peered out again.

There was nobody in sight. The area around the boulders was deserted. So was the top of the ridge. The armed frogmen had disappeared.

The remaining cadets sat up. They looked grim. Hardly surprising, Max thought.

'What now?' Abby asked.

Max pointed along the ditch towards the cliff edge. 'I'm going to check the cove,' he said, 'see what's happening down there. The rest of you stay here. Keep watch. Let me know if you see anyone.'

If the other cadets objected to Max issuing instructions, they didn't show it. He presumed they were just as shaken as he was by the brutal death of the farmer. He felt sick again as he crawled along the wet ditch. Would he be able to see the farmer's body from here? What would it look like, after falling from such a height?

The ditch fell away sharply when it reached the cliff edge. A small waterfall trickled down the cliff. Max felt a moment of vertigo as he lay on his front, his head millimetres from the edge. It was a very long way down. He took his NV binoculars and scanned the cove.

There was movement down there. It took a moment of focusing to realise what was going on. The frogmen were back on the beach. Max counted thirteen men, and remembered that he had seen thirteen frogmen arriving. From the way a couple of them were waving their arms, they were panicking. Two men ran towards the cliff. They were out of sight for a minute. When they came into view again, they were carrying something.

Max knew what their burden must be. Half of him wanted to avoid looking at it. But he knew he had to.

The farmer's body was whole, at least, and not yet stiff. It slumped in the middle as two frogmen carried it at either end.

'What are they doing?' Max whispered to himself.

It soon became clear.

The frogmen carrying the corpse were the first to enter the ocean. They wore their rebreathers and masks. Max watched them wade in and disappear. He wondered if one of them was the guy with red eyes. Then they disappeared entirely, pulling the corpse under the water with them.

The remaining frogmen followed, six in a line, then five. Within minutes, they had submerged into the South Atlantic, leaving no evidence of their presence on the beach. Max scanned out to sea, searching for any kind of vessel. He saw none. The frogmen had simply disappeared.

He lowered his binoculars and crawled back to the others.

'Well?' Abby said.

'They've gone. They've taken the farmer's body with them.'

'Where to?'

'I don't know. They just . . . disappeared.'

'People don't just disappear, Max.'

'Well, these ones did.'

The rain was heavier than ever. There was a roll of thunder in the distance and, far out to sea, a split of lightning.

'We should get back to the guest house,' Max said, and the others agreed.

The ocean was cold and the current was strong. But the

frogmen had trained in these waters, and they knew what they were doing.

The dead body was a cumbersome cargo. It wanted to float and the two frogmen holding it had to use their weight to keep it submerged. One of them was called Alonzo, but everybody called him Rojo because of the colour of his eyes. He had thrown the man from the clifftop. It had felt good, but now it was his duty to clear up after himself.

He had a bright torch clipped to his diving rig. At first it wasn't much help. It illuminated the murky ocean around him, but all he could see was the dead man's face, his skin pale, his eyes open, his hair waving like tentacles in the water.

They didn't have far to travel. Their underwater transport was close to shore, and it was waiting for them.

The team's minisub was an impressive piece of kit. Even when you'd used it as often as these men had, it was hard not to be awed by its capability. It was a small, sixteen-man submarine, very similar to the vessels used by the American Navy SEALs. The Argentine Navy had kept it a secret that they possessed a fleet of these underwater vehicles.

Perhaps it would not be a secret for long.

This particular minisub was free-flooding. This meant that the interior of the submarine was full of water. Its occupants were required to use either rebreathers, standard scuba gear or on-board oxygen masks to breathe while they were inside it. A grey, bullet-shaped vessel, it opened at the centre to allow the team to enter. Two frogmen were already inside, controlling the vessel. Rojo and his companion manoeuvred the dead body into the sub, strapped themselves and their gear in, and waited for the rest of their team.

They arrived minutes later, the light from their torches announcing their approach. Swiftly, they took their positions in the minisub. The minisub closed up silently, a hard shell encasing the frogmen and their cargo in its belly. Then it started to vibrate, which told Rojo that they were moving.

It was dimly lit inside the sub, and there was a strange quality to sounds: they were muffled and deadened. Rojo stayed very still, preserving his energy in the cold water. It was impossible to tell in which direction they were travelling, or how fast. And it was difficult to track the passing of time. Sometimes a minute felt like an hour down here, or an hour like a minute. He closed his eyes and thought back over the evening's events. Landing in the cove. Climbing to the top of the cliff and putting in surveillance while his unit mates went about their work elsewhere. Hurling the man from the top of the cliff to avoid firing a noisy weapon. And then he remembered searching the clifftop, checking that there was nobody else in the vicinity. A sixth sense had nagged at him, telling him that there was somebody else up here. But so far as he could see, the clifftop had been deserted.

Why, then, could he not shake the feeling that someone else had been watching?

Rojo put the thought from his mind. The minisub had stopped vibrating. That meant they were at their destination. The sub opened up from the centre. Rojo and his companion took hold of the corpse and floated out of the minisub up to the surface of the ocean.

Three rigid inflatable boats – RIBs, as they were known – were waiting for them here, bouncing up and down on the ocean swell. The weather was foul: heavy rain and thunder overhead. But Rojo and his guys were experienced. They'd trained and operated in worse sea conditions than this before. Rojo and his partner were able to move themselves and the corpse to the nearest RIB. A couple of guys in the boat helped them manhandle the body into it, then the rest of the team climbed into the boats. Once they were all accounted for, the RIBs escorted them to a large fishing vessel that was nearby.

It was a sturdy trawler, weather-beaten but stubbornly stable in the stormy ocean. Nobody would have imagined that it played host to a team of Argentine special forces. And that was the point. Rojo's RIB drew up along the starboard side. Two men on the trawler lowered a harness, which Rojo fitted to the corpse before giving the men above a thumbs-up. They hauled the farmer's body up the side of the trawler. It swung in the wind and bounced heavily against the side of the boat, but within thirty seconds it was aboard.

Next, Rojo and his team were hauled up onto the trawler. The decks were wet with spray and men shouted instructions across the bow at the top of their voices, so they could be heard over the wind. A crew member divested Rojo of his rebreather. Rojo noticed the man stare at his red eyes. He glared horribly at him, and the man hurried away. Then Rojo looked around for the body. It was lying ten metres away on the deck, face-down, discarded like a piece of rubbish.

The ship listed suddenly and the body slid further along the deck. Rojo ran over to it, bent down and turned it face upwards. The corpse was already white and bloated. Even Rojo, who had killed his share of men, was revolted. The sooner they got rid of it, the better.

It was not simply a matter of throwing the body out to sea though. If they did that, the tide could wash it up on one of the beaches of the Falkland Islands. Much better for it to disappear without trace. For that, they needed to use a body bag and some weights. As Rojo stood up, he saw his mate bringing exactly that.

The body bag was made of thick plastic with a sturdy zip along the top. The weights – several kilos of rocks – were already inside the bag. Rojo's mate laid it on the ground and removed the rocks. Then they each took one end of the corpse and lifted it onto the bag. The limbs had begun to stiffen. They each took one end of the corpse and stuffed it into the body bag. Rojo's hands were cold, which made the job more difficult, but eventually the corpse was inside. They crammed the rocks back into the bag then tried to zip it up. Rojo remembered going on holiday with his mum and dad as a boy, and how difficult it was to close the zip on their over-full suitcase. The body bag was like that. When the zip was finally closed, Rojo and his mate lifted the bag, each taking one end, and hauled it to the deck railing. It was heavy – the body was a lot more difficult to move out of the water – but with an effort they managed to lift it up over the railings and throw it overboard.

Rojo watched the body bag hit the water then sink. Out of sight forever.

He scowled. It had been a long, difficult night. He was freezing. He headed below decks to find something to eat.

7

War and Peace

Max woke the next morning to the raucous sound of seabirds.

At first, his mind numbed by sleepiness, he thought he'd dreamed it all. The trek across the island to the cove. The frogmen. The murder. He fully expected, when he opened his eyes, to find himself in the dormitory at Valley House. But as he came to, he realised that the window was not where he expected it to be, that it was lighter in the room than usual, and that there was an unfamiliar mound next to his bed. Forcing his eyes open a little wider, he saw that it was his foul-weather gear from last night, piled in a heap where he'd left it in his eagerness to put his head on his pillow. That in turn made him imagine Hector's voice, barking a reprimand for not tidying his gear when he'd finished with it. Slightly guiltily, Max forced himself to get up. He sat, bleary-eyed, on the edge of his bed.

The clock on his bedside table told him it was three

minutes to seven. It had been almost four o'clock by the time they'd sneaked back into the guest house and crawled into bed. Three hours of sleep after a night like that was nowhere near enough. Max gave serious consideration to the idea of going back to bed. Two things stopped him: the knowledge that if they were to keep their cover, they had a daytime schedule to adhere to; and the smell of bacon. Max found himself wondering, as he pulled on some clothes, if he could detect sausage too. He decided he could. His stomach urged him to get a move on.

Two minutes later, he was in the dining room. Lukas, Lili, Abby and Sami were already there, plates of cooked breakfast in front of them. Abby was shovelling hers in as if worried somebody might steal the food from in front of her. The others were eating more sedately. All of them, however, had dark rings under their eyes and a haunted expression.

'We need to . . .' Max started to say, but he was cut off mid-sentence by the arrival of Arlene, the woman who ran the guest house. She was carrying a plate of sausage, bacon, egg and tomato, which she placed on the table.

'We wondered if we'd ever be seeing you, dearie,' she said.

'Right,' Max said, putting his hand through his ruffled hair. 'Overslept, I guess.' He sat down at the table and picked up his knife and fork.

'I can't help wondering what you were up to last night,' Arlene said.

The cadets studiously concentrated on their breakfasts. For a moment, the only sound was that of cutlery against china.

'What do you mean?' Max asked carefully.

'Well, you look like you've hardly slept. Midnight feasts, was it?' Arlene chuckled to herself and pottered out of the room.

'Wish it *was* midnight feasts,' Abby muttered, before cramming another forkful of bacon into her mouth. Max fell hungrily on his breakfast. He didn't say a word until his plate was clean. 'We should get in touch with the Watchers,' he said quietly, one eye on the door. 'They need to know what we saw last night.'

'And we should be more careful,' Lukas added. 'Those frogmen could easily have seen us. We'd have gone the same way as the farmer.'

The others nodded grimly.

'I'll make the call,' Max said. 'Let's meet outside in twenty minutes.' He frowned. 'Hector's going to freak out that we didn't get any photographs.'

Back up in his bedroom, Max locked the door from the inside and retrieved the encrypted satellite phone from the suitcase under his bed. He dialled the number that he had committed to memory. The call was answered immediately. Hector's voice sounded distant. As usual, he dispensed with pleasantries.

– I told you only to get in touch if you had something to report.

'Which is why I'm calling,' Max replied, and he proceeded to explain exactly what they'd seen.

Hector listened in silence. Only when Max was finished did he ask any questions.

– Did you get photographs?

Max hesitated. 'Negative,' he said. 'We were going to, but then the farmer turned up and . . . I'm sorry. We messed up. It won't happen again.' Max knew there was no point being anything other than straightforward with Hector. *If you make a mistake on ops,* he had often said, *own it. That's the only way you earn the respect of your colleagues.*

And Hector was true to his word. There was a small pause, then he carried on as if Max hadn't even mentioned the mess-up.

– *You sure you didn't see any vessels out at sea, either dropping off the frogmen or picking them up?*

'Nothing,' Max said. 'Could there be, I don't know, submarines operating in these waters?'

– *It's possible. But they'd need some advanced technology to get that close to the shore. There's a type of vessel called a minisub. We didn't think that the Argentine military had any, but we've been wrong about stuff like that before . . .*

'They killed someone, Hector,' Max said. His voice shook as he said it, and he realised how traumatised he'd been by the sight. It was not the first time he'd seen somebody die, but it was certainly the most pointless death he'd ever witnessed.

– *They'll kill a lot more if we don't stop them. I'm going to recommend to the Ministry of Defence that we put the Falklands on a war footing. But that will take time to filter up to the Prime Minister, and we have to watch our step. If the mole at RAF Mount Pleasant gets wind of this, it could spark an immediate attack.*

'What should we do?'

– Keep up your surveillance. Right now, any pieces of information you can gather could mean the difference between war and peace. And Max?

'Yeah?'

You have cameras. Use them.

Before Max could say anything else, Hector had hung up.

He sat on the edge of his bed, holding the sat phone. It seemed absurd to him that a teenager sitting in a chintzy guest-house bedroom, thousands of miles from home, could be in such a responsible position. But that was his life now. Deep down, he wouldn't have it any other way.

He put on warm layers of clothing and met the cadets outside. Quickly, he relayed to them his conversation with Hector.

'War and peace, hey?' Abby said. 'No pressure then.' But she didn't have the usual light-hearted catch in her voice. It was difficult to see a man killed one night and be all jokey the next morning.

Today's activity was birdwatching. They were due to meet a local expert down by the harbour at nine o'clock. They knew that his name was Peter, but they hadn't yet met him. As soon as they approached the harbour, however, it was easy to identify him.

Peter was a man in his sixties, with thinning hair and a narrow, hawkish face. He stood by the concrete pier where two fishing boats and a thirty-two-foot yacht were moored. He was dressed for the outdoors in a heavy coat. Over one shoulder he carried several pairs of binoculars and over the other a rucksack. He held up some walkers' maps in protective plastic coverings. He nodded to the cadets as they approached, and held up a hand to attract their attention. 'Greetings!' he called to them. 'Are you my young guests?'

'Greetings?' Abby muttered. 'Who says "greetings" these days?' But the cadets smiled and waved. When they reached Peter, they all shook hands.

'We've picked a splendid day for it,' Peter said. He raised one hand to the sky, which was clear blue with only a few drifting clouds. 'Stiff old breeze, but last night's storm has passed. I predict a successful excursion. Shall we go? My car is ten minutes' walk away.' He set off at a brisk pace along the harbour. 'We can expect cormorants and oystercatchers, and I know an excellent spot for king penguins. If we're lucky, we might see a turkey vulture, but don't hold me to that, chaps.' He grinned at them. 'And chapesses. You've seen this, of course?'

They had stopped by a stone obelisk, with a bronze statue atop it. Behind the obelisk was a large house with a green roof flying a union flag. Written on the obelisk were the words:

In memory of those who liberated us
14 June 1982

'The war memorial,' Peter said. 'That's Government House behind it, where the governor lives. And if you read these plaques surrounding the memorial, you'll see the names of the two hundred and fifty-five British soldiers who lost their lives during the war.' He nodded respectfully at the memorial, like a priest bowing at an altar, while the cadets stood silently around him. 'We live in hope,' he said quietly, 'that nobody else will ever have to lose their lives in a dispute over our islands.'

The cadets glanced at each other, but said nothing.

Peter's vehicle was an old Land Rover with rickety suspension. He drove it sedately out of Stanley, along the road the cadets had followed the previous night. Where the cadets had gone cross-country, however, Peter continued along a narrow road that headed inland to the west. The land on either side was flat and grassy. There was no sign of human habitation. After driving for ten minutes, Peter pulled over by the side of the road and killed the engine. 'A word of warning, chaps and chapesses,' he said, turning in his seat so he could see them all. 'There are certain parts of the island, especially in this area, where we can't set foot. During the war, anti-personnel mines were planted all across the island. Most of them have been located, decommissioned and removed. But areas remain where it is too difficult to find or approach the mines. These areas have been cordoned off with wire fencing, and there are minefield warning signs, so naturally nobody goes there any more.'

'That's terrible,' Lili said.

'Every cloud has a silver lining,' Peter replied, waving a finger. 'For the keen nature-watcher – and for we ornithologists in particular – these minefields are fascinating places. No human has set foot on them for nearly forty years. And as humans are nature's greatest enemy, these areas have become miniature nature reserves, rich habitats for all manner of creature, especially birds. They're too light to trigger the landmines, you see.'

'Are you telling us we're going on a nature ramble in a minefield?' Lukas said.

'Not *in* a minefield, my dear chap. But close to a minefield. I'm sure I don't need to say this, but please pay attention to any exclusion fences and warning signs you see. Let's make sure you get back to Arlene's in one piece.'

'You know Arlene?' Abby asked.

'Everyone knows Arlene,' Peter said.

Outside the vehicle, Peter handed around the binoculars and maps. The cadets politely listened to his explanation of how to use them, though it was quite unnecessary. Then he pointed in a northerly direction and set off across the grassland. The cadets followed.

It was good to be out in the open air. The breeze felt as if it was blowing away some of the shock of the night before. As they climbed a shallow knoll, however, and the ocean came into view in the distance, the memory of the frogmen and the corpse hit Max with great clarity, and he had to repress a shudder.

They walked for twenty minutes before Peter stopped and pointed to their ten o'clock. 'Over there,' he said.

Max and the others raised their binoculars. A couple of hundred metres away was a wire fence and a post with a red sign: 'Danger: Mines'. The fence extended as far as Max could see. The land beyond was not much different but, even as they looked, a flock of birds suddenly rose into the air. Max couldn't help smiling as he watched them swoop and dive in formation. When he lowered his binoculars, he saw Sami grinning broadly while the others continued to watch, clearly rapt.

'Skuas!' Peter announced. 'See the white markings on their wings? Tricky little chaps. They're kleptoparasites. That means they'll chase other birds and steal their prey. They're not averse to killing and eating other birds either. Aggressive, dangerous – but beautiful too.'

'A bit like Angel,' Abby said under her breath.

'Like whom, my dear?'

'Just a friend,' Abby replied. 'Can we get a bit closer?'

'Of course. Just don't –'

'Walk into the minefield. Yeah, don't worry. I'm quite attached to my limbs.'

As they headed across the grass towards the minefield, the flock of skuas melted away. Excitedly, Peter pointed to another bird, perched on a fence post. 'Cormorant,' he announced. The bird flew away. Max found himself swept up in the guide's excitement. He scanned the area for birds as carefully as he had scanned for enemies the previous night. He wasn't disappointed. Flocks rose in the distance. Solitary birds stood on fence posts and pecked busily around the grass. For the briefest moment, Max felt as if he was back at the children's home where he had been raised. Then, he would escape into nature at any opportunity. It awed him and comforted him at the same time. It did the same now.

By the time they reached the edge of the minefield, Max understood what Peter had been telling them. This truly was a birder's paradise. The minefield itself was peaceful and rather beautiful. Only the fence and the ugly red sign gave any indication that it was a potentially fatal site. The cadets wandered up and down the fence, binoculars glued to their eyes. Max scanned the horizon, watching the birds rise and swoop. One in particular caught his eye. A vulture, maybe, but he didn't want to stop looking to ask Peter. He followed its line of flight as it headed south, over the boundary of the minefield and off towards the horizon.

Then he saw something else.

It was hard to estimate how far away it was. Somewhere between seven hundred and fifty metres and a kilometre, he reckoned, and it was only visible from this position because they were standing on higher ground. It was a long, squat, grey building, possibly constructed from concrete. A bleak-looking place, seemingly deserted, and with no road leading to it.

He sensed Peter standing next to him. 'What's that building?' he asked, lowering his binoculars and pointing in that direction.

'Ah, that's just the old listening post,' Peter said.

'A what?'

'You seem more interested in that than in the birds, young man.'

'No,' Max said, 'not really. Just curious, is all. What's a listening post?'

'Well, I'm no military tactician,' Peter said. 'But my understanding is that it's a radar station. It detects aircraft flying overhead. If they're on an unexpected flight path, the people at RAF Mount Pleasant are put on high alert.'

'You mean it looks out for enemy planes.'

'I suppose I do. Now then, I'm very hopeful that we might get a glimpse of a black-browed albatross –'

'Would you mind if I went for a bit of a wander?' Max said.

Peter blinked. 'I . . . well, I suppose not.'

Max smiled at him. 'I find it peaceful to be by myself sometimes. You know?' As he spoke, Sami approached. 'Sami and the others will stay around here, I'm sure. Won't you, Sami?'

'Of course,' Sami said, one eyebrow raised. And when Peter moved away, he said, 'What's going on?'

'There's a radar station over there,' Max said. 'I want to check it out. Can you and the others keep Peter occupied?'

Sami gave a serious nod. 'I will ask him about penguins,' he said. 'I think he will talk about them for a very long time.'

'I think you might be right.'

Sami followed Peter. Max turned and headed to the listening post.

8

Albatross

The sound of the other cadets talking receded as Max strolled in the direction of the listening post. After a couple of minutes, when he was out of sight, he started to jog. He kept going to the barbed-wire cordon around the minefield. Occasionally flocks of birds startled into the sky, disturbed by his presence. Max didn't stop to admire them. The listening post was his focus. He hurried towards it.

There was a thin film of sweat on his forehead by the time he had to stop. The barbed-wire fence around the minefield to his right met a more substantial fence that surrounded the listening post. This perimeter fence was about fifty metres from the low concrete building itself, but it had no minefield warnings attached to it. Did that mean it was safe to pass? Max didn't know. It certainly wasn't *easy* to pass. The fence was a good two metres high and topped with a roll of razor wire. It was impassable – without the aid of cutting tools.

To his left he thought he could see a bulge in the fence about thirty metres along. He checked back over his shoulder to ensure he was still unobserved, then jogged along beside the fence. He saw that the fence had been cut. The wire mesh curled back on itself, creating a gap large enough for an adult to pass through. Max examined the grass: it was flattened, which suggested that somebody had recently walked this way. Something else caught his eye. A fragment of black material was caught on the mesh of the fence. Max carefully removed it: just a scrap, but it had a slight elasticity. He couldn't be certain, but he felt pretty confident that it came from a neoprene dive suit. At least one frogman, he decided, had penetrated the fence recently.

He peered through the gap in the fence towards the listening post. It was a bleak, desolate place. Max had the impression that it was seldom visited. It crossed his mind that there could be a very good reason for this: landmines. It was, after all, cordoned off.

But someone had passed this way without triggering an explosion. If they'd done it, perhaps Max could do it too. His eyes followed the line of flattened grass. If he kept to it, he would be able to avoid danger. And then, maybe, he could find out what the frogmen had been doing here at the listening station.

He took a deep breath, then gingerly stepped through the hole in the fence.

'Where's Max?' Abby spoke under her breath, so that Peter wouldn't hear her.

Sami replied in a whisper: 'He's gone to check something out. We need to keep Peter occupied so he doesn't wander in that direction.'

Peter needed no help staying busy. His binoculars seemed glued to his face. He was watching another flock of skuas swooping over the minefield. His binoculars followed them like spectators watching the ball at a tennis match. At one point he cooed in delight – for a moment Sami thought the sound had come from a nearby bird. When he lowered his binoculars, he seemed surprised to see the cadets standing around him in a semicircle, watching him.

'Is everything okay, chaps and chapesses?'

Before he could answer, something dark swooped overhead, casting a shadow over them. Peter looked up and his face creased with pleasure. 'A black-browed albatross,' he announced, pointing at the bird. 'Endangered, you know. Beautiful birds. We're lucky to see one.'

The albatross settled on the ground in the minefield, no more than thirty metres from its audience. Peter and the cadets stood very still.

'Some people – sailors, mostly – say that the albatross brings bad luck. I pay no attention to them.'

The albatross cocked his head in their direction, as if it was listening to them.

'Ever get the feeling you're being watched?' Abby said. The bird suddenly took flight again. It circled several times above them and they craned their necks to watch it. Then it flew, along the minefield cordon, in the direction Max had gone.

'Come on!' Peter called. His voice throbbed with excitement and he started running after the albatross, like a puppy chasing a ball. The sight of the bird seemed to have taken years off him.

'Hey, Peter!' Sami called. 'Why don't we just stay around here –'

But Peter either didn't hear or was ignoring him. He continued to run after the albatross.

'I told Max we'd keep him occupied while he checks out the listening post,' Sami hissed. 'Come on!'

The cadets ran after their eager instructor, who showed no sign of slowing down.

The moment he climbed through the hole in the fence, Max's skin tingled with anxiety. Each step he took felt reckless. He found himself feeling the ground with the sole of his foot before putting any real pressure on it, but he told himself that was ridiculous. If a landmine was hidden, it was hidden. He wouldn't feel it before stepping on it.

Much better, he decided, to stick to his original plan and follow the existing path across the grass. It was definitely there – a faint indentation in the grass. He followed it for a while in the direction of the concrete building, but then it seemed to disappear into nowhere. Max looked around for any more flattened grass, but there was nothing. Just grass, ankle height, swaying gently in the breeze.

Decision time: advance or retreat? He felt a chill at the prospect of crossing a potential minefield to reach the building, but also the urge to keep moving. If the frogmen had wanted to come here, there had to be a reason . . .

Keep going, he told himself. *It's worth the risk.*

He looked up. Was that an albatross overhead? He remembered reading that they were considered bad luck by superstitious types.

But Max wasn't one of those. He raised one foot.

'WHAT ON EARTH DO YOU THINK YOU'RE DOING?'

Max spun around. Peter was running along the perimeter fence of the listening post towards the hole in the fence. The other cadets were following him, Sami waving his arms around in an apologetic way. For a moment, Max felt deeply frustrated with his good friend, but Sami looked so distressed that Max couldn't keep it up for long.

Peter was red-faced and clearly very angry. He stopped by the hole in the fence. 'Get back here *now*, young man!' he ordered. Max hesitated, but he understood that he had no real option. He retraced his steps back to the hole in the fence.

'Did you do this?' Peter demanded, indicating the hole.

Max was about to deny it, but something stopped him. If he said it wasn't him, would Peter inform the authorities about it? What would happen then? Would it become common knowledge that something sinister was happening? Max predicted that Hector wouldn't want that. 'I . . . I just wanted to get a closer look,' he said, hanging his head sheepishly. He hoped Peter wouldn't ask *how* he'd cut through the wire.

'I can't believe you could be so irresponsible,' Peter said. 'You seemed like a perfectly sensible young man, and I thought we were having a lovely day.' He turned to the other cadets, who were standing in a group behind him, keeping quiet. 'Come along, all of you. We're going back to the car. Our day's birdwatching is at an end.'

He strode away towards the Land Rover. He'd only taken a few paces when he stopped and looked back over his shoulder. 'Well, come on then!' he said.

The cadets followed. Max sensed that they were bursting with questions, but they couldn't ask them while they were in earshot of Peter. So they kept quiet as they walked back to the vehicle.

Clouds were coming in from the sea. The temperature was dropping. By the time they reached the Land Rover, it was completely overcast. Wordlessly, Peter unlocked the vehicle and took the wheel as the cadets climbed in. Max sat in the passenger seat. As Peter drove off, the atmosphere was thick with tension.

They were back on the road to Stanley before anyone spoke. It was Max. 'I was just wondering . . .'

'What?' Peter snapped.

'I was just wondering if there were mines in the area around the listening post.'

'Did you see any minefield signs?'

'No,' Max said. 'Not on that bit of fence.'

'Well, there you go,' Peter said. 'But that doesn't mean you should have been in there.'

'No,' Max muttered. 'I'm sorry.'

As he said it, he glanced in the rear-view mirror to see the other cadets staring at his reflection. Did they know what he was thinking? That tonight, when it was dark, he would return to the listening post to try to find out more?

Their steely expressions suggested that they did.

Silently, they trundled back to the capital.

9

Click

'We should split up,' Lili said.

They were back in the guest house, having said a chilly goodbye to Peter at the harbour. Arlene had fed them large helpings of ham and eggs. Now they were in Max's room.

'Some of us should watch the cove,' Lili continued, 'and some of us should examine the listening post.' She frowned. 'I have a feeling this could be our last night in the Falklands. If Hector's right, and the islands are going to be put on a war footing, they won't need us here any longer. We should do everything we can to gather as much intelligence as possible while we're here.'

'We'll need to be more careful than last night,' Lukas said. 'We could have got killed. It was stupid.'

'I say we watch the top of the cove from a distance,' Abby suggested. 'We don't need to see the frogmen landing. We need to see what they're doing once they get onto the island.'

'Roger that,' Max said. He thought for a minute. 'Lukas

and I will go to the listening post. The rest of you put in surveillance on the clifftop.'

'What do you think you'll find there?' Sami said. 'At the listening post, I mean.'

'I don't know,' Max said. 'But if the frogmen were there, I don't think they were just sightseeing.'

The cadets nodded grimly.

Once more, they waited until Arlene was in bed before creeping out of the guest house and heading away from the town. The weather was clearer tonight, the moon brighter. That was a blessing and a curse: it was easier to see by a bright moon, but also easier to *be* seen. They followed the same road out of Stanley as the previous night. At the end of it, however, they split up. Abby, Lili and Sami followed the usual route cross-country to the clifftop. Max and Lukas headed in the opposite direction.

The two friends were silent as they jogged across the grassy ground. Although the night was clear, the area was exposed to the wind. Its howl drowned out all other sounds. The moon cast long shadows ahead of them. Aware that they were exposed, and that their sense of hearing was compromised, they stopped every minute to check that nobody was watching them. As far as they could see, they were alone in this wild landscape.

They had been jogging for ten minutes when, over to their eleven o'clock, they saw the jagged outline of the minefield fence darkly visible against the night sky. Max found it chilling to think of all those landmines, lying silently dormant for decades, ready to explode, maim and kill at the slightest pressure. He thought he could see the outline of a bird perched on one of the upright posts.

'It's the albatross,' Lukas said quietly. 'That Peter guy said they were bad luck.'

Max shivered. 'There's no such thing,' he said quietly. 'We make our own luck, right?'

'Right.'

'Then let's keep moving.'

It took them another ten minutes to reach the gap in the fence. Here they paused again and looked around. No sign of movement or personnel. 'I think you should keep guard here,' Max said quietly. 'If you see anybody approaching . . .'

'. . . I'll let you know.' Lukas nodded and his eyes narrowed as he started to scan the surrounding countryside.

Max took a deep breath. Peter had said that there were no mines around the listening post, but still . . . He trod as lightly as he could as he climbed through the fence and started across the field.

Standing behind the boulders at the cliff edge, Abby, Lili and Sami agreed to split up.

Sami would take up position at the end of the ditch that led to the cliff edge, from where Max had watched the cove the previous night. He would be well hidden there, and could monitor the presence and movement of any vessels out at sea, should they arrive. Lili would hide in a sturdy gorse thicket twenty metres from the top of the ridge that led from the cove: a dense, uncomfortable place, full of thorns and foliage, where nobody else would venture. From here, she could watch – and count – any frogmen coming up the ridge onto the clifftop.

'And I'll head over there,' Abby said, pointing beyond the ditch to a small copse a good three hundred metres away, perched precariously on the clifftop. There were few trees on the island, and Abby wondered how these trees had survived in such an exposed and windswept position. Then she thought that they were an obvious landmark, rather like the boulders.

'Why there?' Sami said.

Abby frowned. 'I've got a theory,' she said. 'Those frogmen had heavy rucksacks, right?'

'Sure, but –'

'Hear me out. So far as we can tell, they haven't been staying on the islands. They've been coming ashore and then leaving the same night. If they were staying, and needed a load of survival gear, I'd understand the rucksacks. But if they're only here for a few hours . . .'

Lili nodded. 'Maybe they're bringing stuff onto the island and hiding it.'

'Right,' Abby said.

'What sort of stuff?' Sami asked.

'I guess that's what we need to find out,' Abby said. 'But if I was going to hide something, I'd probably choose somewhere I could easily describe to the person who needs to find it again. I'd choose some kind of landmark.' She put one hand on the nearest boulder. 'These are a bit too exposed,' she said. 'The ditch is a possibility, I guess. But those trees . . .'

Sami put a tentative arm on Abby's shoulder. 'You must make sure you aren't seen,' he said.

Abby allowed herself a grin. 'I'll make a point of it,' she said.

They separated. Abby ran along the cliff, far enough back from the clifftop that she wouldn't be seen from below. Her arm ached. There was always some pain there – a souvenir from a brush with an MP5 round on a previous mission – but tonight it was worse than normal. A dull throb seemed to penetrate right down to the bone, like a warning.

She told herself to put it out of her mind, to think of something else. Her thoughts turned, as they so often did, to Max. It was no secret – between Abby and Max or indeed among the other cadets – that her feelings for him were more than friendly. Did he feel the same way? It was hard to tell. They had agreed that nothing could ever happen between them. The Watchers, they knew, wouldn't allow it. But that didn't mean they couldn't indulge in a flirtatious smile now and again, did it? Apparently so. Solemn, serious Max seemed completely focused on their job, and had no time for her.

Or maybe, she told herself, he was just a good actor.

Abby snapped her attention back to the job in hand. She was approaching the copse. It was much bigger up close. The trees loomed threateningly above her. She stopped at the treeline for a moment, catching her breath and looking out to sea. The moon cast a silver reflection over the waves and the stars were beautifully bright. It was with a small pang of regret that she plunged into the darkness of the trees.

She could hear branches creaking in the wind, leaves whispering. The ground was softer underfoot. She paused to allow her eyes to adjust to this different quality of darkness. Then she moved further into the copse and started to examine the trees themselves. The trunks were gnarled and twisted, but their bark was smooth. They were mostly unsuitable for climbing. In the heart of the copse, however, was a tree whose trunk was fat at the base but tapered sharply as it rose, with branches protruding at just the right intervals.

Abby climbed it easily. Within seconds she was crouched on a branch among the whispering foliage, a dark figure, invisible – or so she hoped – from the ground. It was uncomfortable, but a good vantage point from which she had a decent view across much of the copse.

It was a gamble. The frogmen might not come anywhere near this place. If they did, there was a chance she would be spotted. But she was willing to take that risk.

She waited.

Max was not hot, but he was sweating heavily by the time he reached the listening station. He touched the cool concrete with one hand, then looked back the way he'd come. He couldn't see Lukas. It made him feel quite alone.

Now that he was at the building, he realised he didn't really know what he was searching for. He knew, from seeing it at a distance, that it was a squat rectangular structure. He supposed there must be an entrance somewhere, but he hadn't seen one yet. He decided to move stealthily around the building and see what was on the far side.

He took one step along the external wall, then stopped. Had he just heard something? A movement?

He held his breath, remained very still and listened hard. Nothing.

His pulse was beating hard as, concealed by the shadow cast by the listening post, he crept along the external wall towards the nearest corner.

Sami had been in place at the top of the cliff for a scant ten minutes when they arrived.

The frogmen emerged from the sea in a spookily neat formation. Three men first, in a line. When they hit the sand they spread out, their rifles raised, then two more lines of five men emerged from the ocean. They all had heavy rebreather masks and bulky rucksacks. Sami knew they couldn't have swum far with all that gear. He tried to spot a vessel out to sea, but saw nothing. Max had said that Hector suspected minisubs. Sami was certain he was right.

He raised his camera and focused it on the emerging frogmen.

Click.

Their arrival was now a matter of record.

The frogmen didn't remain on the beach for long. They removed their rebreathing apparatus and stowed it somewhere Sami couldn't see, against the cliff. Then they headed in a line towards the ridge that led to the clifftop, out of Sami's line of sight.

He hunkered down, still and hidden, hoping that Lili was well concealed.

* * *

The thicket in which Lili was hidden was so dense that if she moved even a millimetre, a thorn would scratch her. So she put herself in a position such that her camera was raised, balanced on a sturdy twig, and pointing towards the top of the ridge. And then she stayed very still.

Which meant that, when the frogmen appeared, marching in single file along the ridge, their heavy rucksacks on their backs, they plainly had no idea she was there.

She counted them: thirteen men. They were clearly fit and strong, because the climb seemed to have had no physical effect on them. Each was armed with a suppressed assault rifle, and they all had bulky rucksacks. Lili wondered what they contained.

Click.

Click.

Click.

She froze. One of the frogmen had stopped and turned. He was looking in her direction, his head cocked, a suspicious expression on his face. Her muscles tensed. She held her breath.

Time seemed to stand still.

Then the frogman shook his head and turned away again.

They marched on.

Lili remained still.

Abby was growing cold and uncomfortable. The wind was blowing harder and she had to grip the tree trunk more tightly. Her muscles ached, and she was beginning to lose confidence in her plan. What if the frogmen didn't come this way?

This was foolish, she decided. She should get down, move to the edge of the copse and see if she could catch sight of anyone in the vicinity. She unwrapped one arm from around the tree trunk.

Then she froze.

She saw the movement in her peripheral vision to her right. She didn't dare turn her head. Holding her breath, she stayed absolutely still. The figure on the edge of her vision came closer. She could see him now, and his four companions. They were heading in her direction, hauling heavy, bulky rucksacks. They came to a halt directly under Abby's tree.

Abby exhaled very slowly. She knew that if she allowed herself even the slightest movement, there was a risk that the men might see her.

They spoke. Gruff voices, unintelligible to Abby. Each of them lowered their rucksack to the ground. Two of them withdrew objects which Abby couldn't quite make out at first. Only when they unfolded them did she see that they were collapsible entrenching tools. Or, as Abby would have called them before joining the Special Forces Cadets, spades.

The two men started to dig. The dull thud of their entrenching tools hitting the ground was slow and metronomic. The other three men stood guard, their weapons slung across their chests as they peered through the trees, checking that nobody was approaching. None of them, however, thought to look up. So they didn't see Abby, watching them carefully.

Max had his back pressed up against the concrete external

wall of the listening station. He was at the corner of the building, listening hard.

No sound.

He turned the corner.

This end of the building was still in shadow. The external wall remained featureless. No windows, no door. Max moved along it in the darkness, his footsteps making no sound. He reached the next corner, listened, then turned.

He was exposed to the moonlight now. It was bright enough to make him squint. Five metres from his position there was a door. He crept towards it. It was sturdy and strong, made of painted iron. And it was locked. There was no way in.

To its left, however, he noticed something.

There was a concrete block by the door: a cube about two metres long. On its nearest side was a metal grille. Max took it to be a housing of some sort. Maybe there was a generator inside, or some kind of plumbing. Whatever it was, a dim red light glowed between the block and the external wall of the listening station.

He moved towards it, his pulse racing.

The red light originated from a box fixed to the back of the concrete cube. It was black and about the size of a cereal packet. Max knelt down to examine it. A panel, just next to the light, read: 'Mode S Transponder'.

He blinked and frowned. He knew what a transponder was: a device to receive and transmit radio signals. Was this part of the listening station's apparatus? He didn't think so. Why would it be fastened to this concrete cube like an afterthought? It was obviously powered by battery as there were no cables leading into it. And it was new. Or at least not weathered, as it would be if it had been outside for a long time.

No. This was a recent addition. And he suddenly knew, with cold certainty, why it was here. The transponder had surely been deployed to relay the precise position of the listening station to enemy aircraft. Because in the event of an attack, this listening post – the purpose of which was to track enemy aircraft – would be a prime target for immediate destruction.

Max pulled his camera from his pocket.

Click.

Click.

Click.

He stowed the camera again and stood up. He decided that he should destroy the transponder immediately. Nobody knew when the Argentine attack might take place. It could be any time. It could even be tonight. This transponder was a crucial piece of kit in the enemy's arsenal. It had to go.

He raised his right leg and rested his heel against the corner of the transponder, ready to strike it hard.

And then he saw it.

The shadow.

Someone was behind him.

Max's blood froze. He felt as though all the strength had drained from his limbs. It occurred to him, momentarily, that it might be Lukas. But he knew it wasn't. Lukas wouldn't creep up on him like that. He'd have made his presence known. This was someone else.

And Max had to prepare to fight him.

He drew a breath, summoned his strength, and turned around.

He immediately saw that it was one of the frogmen. He wore a wetsuit and his hair was still damp. He was clutching his weapon – an assault rifle – broadside on, by the barrel and the butt. He was clearly unwilling to fire it, but that didn't mean he couldn't do some damage. He snarled as he lunged towards Max, thrusting the side of the weapon into Max's face.

Max was fast. He feinted to the right and the weapon passed over his head. Max jabbed his left elbow hard into his attacker's gut. He heard a gasp as the frogman, winded, doubled over in pain. Pivoting on his left foot, Max spun around, his right leg extended, and kicked the back of the frogman's left knee. The man collapsed into a kneeling position, giving Max the opportunity to do the one thing he needed to do.

Run.

He sprinted to the corner of the listening post, intending to retrace his steps back to Lukas.

Lukas.

Max suddenly realised that if the frogman had managed to creep up on him, Lukas must be in trouble. That thought was enough to make him hesitate as he turned the corner.

And that moment of hesitation was his big mistake.

A second frogman was waiting for him. It was not only his presence that chilled Max, it was his red eyes. This was the guy who had murdered the old man last night. He too was using his weapon as a cudgel, and he attacked Max with the butt end. It slammed hard into Max's forehead, the impact increased by Max's momentum. The pain was sudden and sharp. Max staggered back, the world spinning. He felt another blow to his face.

He tried to call for Lukas, but then there was a third blow. It cracked into the side of his face and knocked Max, unconscious, to the ground.

When he woke – it could only have been moments later – all he knew at first was that he was moving. He could see the grass bouncing below him. His head was in agony. He wanted to vomit. His wrists were tied behind his back and his ankles were bound. A rag had been shoved into his mouth to keep him quiet. He was being carried backwards over somebody's shoulder.

It hurt to engage his core muscles to look up. But he did it and saw, behind him and to his right, another frogman with another figure slung over his shoulder. Max knew it was Lukas, but he couldn't tell if his friend was conscious or not. And frankly, right now, that was the least of his worries. He had the urge to vomit again, but knew he mustn't because if he puked with the rag shoved in his mouth, he could choke. He mastered the urge, but then the world started spinning once more and he had to close his eyes to get rid of the nausea.

Seconds later, he had passed out again.

10

Stinger

It took a long time for the frogmen in the copse to dig the hole. The ground was clearly very hard and there was a frequent chinking sound as the entrenching tools hit stones. Abby's muscles shrieked, begging her to move, but she didn't dare to. The way the gunmen prowled around the copse told her that they meant business.

Slowly, the hole began to take shape. The diggers had been going for twenty minutes when Abby realised, with a chill, that the hole was coffin-shaped. A horrible thought occurred to her. Were they planning to bury someone? Had there been another death?

Her mind turned to the other cadets. She felt a moment of panic and experienced the urge to climb down and check on them. But of course, that wasn't an option. All she could do was wait and watch as the coffin-shaped hole grew deeper and deeper . . .

* * *

Lili had a rising feeling of unease. The frogmen had filed out of sight, but the memory of the man who had looked towards the thicket where she was hiding was hot in her mind. If he returned that way – and he surely would – there was a high chance that he would check Lili's hiding place.

So she had to move.

It was a painful business, removing herself from the thorny thicket. Her hands and face were scratched and sore by the time she was free. Lili couldn't worry about that. Scanning the area carefully, she crouched low and ran-walked away from the thicket, past the mouth of the ridge, towards the cliff edge. The wind blew her hair wildly as she kept a lookout for any sign of frogmen.

There was none.

Where were they? What were they doing?

Lili couldn't answer those questions, but she knew she needed to hide again. And so she ran to the boulders. Here she checked all around her for threats. The area seemed deserted. She ran on towards the ditch where she knew Sami was hiding. She jumped down into it and crawled along it to the cliff edge. 'Sami!' she hissed once she knew she was in earshot. 'It's me!'

Sami seemed to emerge from nowhere. His face was anxious. 'What's wrong?' he whispered. 'What's happened?'

'Nothing,' Lili said. 'It's okay. I just got worried that one of them might have seen me. I didn't want them to come sniffing around when they return to the cove.'

'What are they doing now?' Sami said.

Lili frowned. 'I don't know,' she said. 'I couldn't see any of them on my way here.'

Sami suddenly seemed a little more steely. 'I think we need to check on the others,' he said.

He began to stand up, but Lili grasped him by the arm. 'No,' she said. 'We need to trust them to do their job. And we need to stay hidden.'

Sami crouched down again with obvious reluctance. 'Something's not right,' he said. 'I can feel it.'

They fell silent.

It was hard for Abby to estimate the depth of the hole from her vantage point above it. About a metre, she reckoned, maybe a little less. Certainly wide enough and deep enough for a body.

But whose?

She couldn't help thinking of her fellow cadets. Where were they? What were they doing? Could this hole be for one of them?

And inevitably, the face in her mind's eye was Max's. It was pale and lifeless. The thought was too painful for her to bear.

Then, as her eyes shot open again, she cursed inwardly. The men below had stopped digging and were looking around, as though they had sensed someone watching them. An icy chill crept through Abby's veins as she forced herself back into stillness. The two men exchanged a glance and shrugged. One of them threw his entrenching tool to the side of the hole, where it settled against the pile of soil they had displaced. The other folded his and placed it on the ground. Then they turned their attention to the four rucksacks that were lying nearby. They each opened one and started to empty it.

It wasn't easy, from this angle and in the darkness, for Abby to get a clear view of the items they took out of the rucksacks. But she soon worked out that they were military. There were weapons and waterproof boxes of ammunition. There were several boxes marked 'C-4', which Abby knew to be a military-grade plastic explosive. There were small flight cases, the contents of which Abby couldn't decipher. There was a large weapon, larger than anything the cadets had ever seen in real life, but which looked like something the Watchers had taught them about: a Stinger. *These are shoulder-mounted surface-to-air missile launchers*, she remembered Angel telling them. *They're designed for men – or women – on the ground to take out aircraft. You cause a lot of destruction with one of these, and take out a lot of people . . .*

The frogmen laid a huge tarpaulin in the hole, with either end spilling out over the edges. Then they started to stash the items on top of it. As soon as the first two rucksacks were empty, they started on the remaining two. In just a couple of minutes, all four rucksacks were empty.

The frogmen folded the tarpaulin over their cache, then started to cover it up again with the loose earth. This was a quick process, but when the hole was filled, there was still a mound of displaced soil. They kicked it flat then found some fallen branches to drag over the cache, removing their footprints and camouflaging the location, at least a little.

When they were finished, they signalled to their companions. Each man retrieved his empty rucksack and slung it over his back. They were clearly preparing to leave when something happened.

One of the frogmen put a finger to his ear and cocked his head. Everything about his body language told Abby that he was listening to something in a comms earpiece. She couldn't see his face, but she could tell, by the low, urgent sound of his voice when he spoke to his companions, that something had happened. Something serious.

They started to move more quickly. As suddenly as they had arrived, they wordlessly melted away into the darkness.

Even when they had gone, Abby barely dared to stir. She clutched the tree, considering what she had just witnessed. The frogmen had been digging in military equipment. She did not doubt what it was for: a cache, a secret store of weapons for ground troops to access if – when – an invasion took place. And the fact that they were doing it now meant the invasion had to be imminent. But that was not foremost in her mind. She had a bad feeling about whatever it was the frogmen had just learned over their comms system.

Something was wrong. She felt bile rise in the back of her throat. Something was *very* wrong.

She climbed back down the tree and fumbled to retrieve her IR camera from inside her coat.

Click.

Click.

When she had photographed the cache and the surrounding area, she stowed the camera again and sprinted back to the treeline. Hidden in the shadows, she looked back across the clifftop. She could see the five frogmen. They had reached the ditch and were crossing it, seemingly unaware that Sami was hiding only a few metres from them. There was no other sign of disturbance. No sign that her fellow cadets were in any kind of danger. She watched the frogmen disappear towards the ridge. Only when the clifftop was deserted again did she venture out from the copse.

Abby ran as hard and as fast as she could, painfully aware that more frogmen could appear at any minute and she risked compromising them all. Her instinct told her this was the right thing to do. She had to check on the others.

A minute later, she was in the ditch, crawling towards the clifftop. 'It's me,' she hissed, to warn Sami of her approach. She was surprised to see him and Lili emerge from the darkness. 'What's going on?'

'I had to leave my OP,' Lili said. 'It's okay – I just thought I'd be safer here.'

'Something's happening,' Abby said, and she quickly recounted to them what she'd just seen.

'That's it,' Sami said. 'I'm going to check on Max and Lukas.'

'Wait,' Lili whispered. She was looking down at the cove. 'Look!'

Several frogmen were by the water's edge already, their rebreathers back on. Others were walking across the beach from the bottom of the ridge. Out to sea, she could just make out the curved top of an underwater vessel.

'Minisub,' she whispered.

'Oh my God,' Lili said. '*Look!*'

Abby returned her attention to the frogmen on the beach. Two of them had something slung over their shoulders.

It took a few seconds for Abby to realise what Lili clearly already knew: it wasn't some*thing*, it was some*one*.

Bile rose once more to the back of her throat. Along with Sami and Lili, she put her binoculars to her eyes and focused in on one of the captives.

She felt sick.

Even from this distance, through IR binoculars, with his head upside down and in profile, she recognised Max's face. She would know it anywhere. It was battered and swollen. Abby couldn't tell if he was awake or not, but he was definitely in a bad way. She panned to the right and saw Lukas in the same position, slung over the shoulder of another man. As Abby watched, the man dumped Lukas on the beach and ran to retrieve his rebreathing gear.

The three cadets lowered their binoculars. Sami was the first to stand. Abby and Lili exchanged a glance. 'There's three of us,' Lili said, 'and fifteen of them.'

'I don't care,' Sami said, and his voice was fiercer than Abby had ever known it.

'They're armed,' Lili said.

'I still don't care. Max and Lukas are our friends. We have to help them.'

'What can we do?' Abby said.

'I don't know yet,' Sami said. 'But what we can't do is stay here and watch.' He turned his back on them and ran along the ditch.

'He's right,' Abby said, getting to her feet. 'Come on.' Without waiting for a reply, she followed Sami.

As a young child, Abby had suffered a recurring nightmare: she wanted to run, but her legs, for some reason, were heavy and useless. She felt like that now: as though, no matter how hard she tried, she simply couldn't run fast enough. In truth, however, the cadets had seldom moved so fast. There was no time for stealth. They hurtled along the clifftop, the moon casting long shadows across the landscape, their hair blowing wildly in the wind. They reached the top of the ridge in a minute and started to make their way down to sea level. The ridge was steep and treacherous. Several times, Abby stumbled and nearly fell. But her leg muscles were strong and her balance and coordination were good – the Watchers had seen to that – so she stayed upright, moving fast. Her mind was whirring. What would they do when they reached the cove? How could they fight the frogmen? How could they rescue Max and Lukas? She didn't know the answer to any of these questions. She only knew one thing: if they didn't get there quickly, they wouldn't be able to help their friends. That thought spurred her on.

But then they reached the bottom of the ridge and burst breathlessly onto the beach, their feet sinking in the sand.

They looked all around.

The beach was empty. There was no sign of Max or Lukas. The only people they could see were two frogmen, many metres out to sea, up to their shoulders in water. Within seconds, they too had disappeared.

They were too late.

The cadets didn't stop running. They hurtled down the beach to the water's edge. Abby wanted to plunge right in, but Lili gripped her from behind and pulled her back. Sami clutched his hair in desperation. Lili had tears streaming down her face. Abby could hardly breathe. She raised one fist in the air and, as she caught her breath, let out a scream of frustration. It hurt her throat and made Lili step back in shock.

The sound of the scream faded as quickly as it started, as though kidnapped by the wind. All that was left on the beach were three teenagers, wet, dishevelled and overcome by panic. They had lost their friends, and could see no way to rescue them.

11

Submerged

Max didn't know if he was dreaming or drowning. Above the water or under it. Alive or dead.

In truth, it was a mixture of them all.

He was only semi-conscious. Awake enough to be aware of the pain and the water flooding in through his nose and mouth, but too groggy to struggle or fight back. One moment he was above the water line, the next he was under, blind and unable to breathe. Whenever he had the opportunity to gasp for air, he felt life surge back into his lungs and muscles, but the longer he was submerged the more he felt consciousness draining from him.

Now, everything was dark. His lungs burned and his head spun. He was buffeted by the currents and choked by the firm grip of his abductor at the back of his neck. He'd been under for thirty seconds, maybe more, and the urge to draw breath was almost overpowering. He was a millisecond away from inhaling a lungful of salt water.

Then, suddenly, he was above the water line again. He gulped great mouthfuls of air, his chest heaving. His sore eyes were open and, for the briefest instant, he had complete clarity. He was on his back and at least thirty metres out to sea. The clifftop was starkly silhouetted by the moon, and he saw people running on the ridge that led down into the cove. He couldn't identify them, but his oxygen-starved brain told him they were his friends.

'Abby . . .' he gasped.

But then he was under again, his lungs only half full of air because he had foolishly spoken.

His few seconds above water had revived him somewhat. He realised that his wrists and ankles were bound. Even if he could struggle away from his abductor, there would be no point. Bizarrely, his firm grip was keeping him alive. And he *was* still alive, he reminded himself – if only just. There had to be a reason. It would have been the easiest thing in the world for the frogmen to kill him.

Maybe it was just that a live body was easier to move than a dead one.

Light. Max winced. It cast straight, opaque beams through the cloudy water. He was aware of bubbles and of black-clad limbs nearby. Before he had time to think anything else, he was being grabbed by the shoulders and the ankles. His lungs had started to burn again and he ached to inhale more air. But he was being dragged further down. Panic gripped him again. He tried to struggle, but his abductors held him fast. There was nothing he could do. His head felt light again. Everything seemed to be moving more slowly. The pain and the panic were subsiding. Everything was spinning silently. His eyes were rolling.

He was on the edge of consciousness.

Then he felt a brutal jolt as his body slammed against something hard. Groggily, he looked around. Beams of light were moving here and there and he realised in his semi-conscious state that they came from handheld underwater torches. One of the frogmen was strapping him to the wall of a hard metallic structure. A mouthpiece of some description was shoved to his face. Oxygen pumped into his mouth and he breathed deeply and gratefully.

Consciousness returned. His breathing apparatus was still in his mouth and his vision was blurry. Lukas was to his left, also strapped in and breathing. The frogmen were fore and aft of them. They were clearly inside an underwater vehicle, roughly cylindrical in shape, although it was too murky and full of seawater for Max to see to the end. Sound was deadened, but he could hear the muffled whine of machinery.

The more oxygen he breathed into his system, the more clarity returned. He could hear Hector's voice in his head. *There's a type of vessel called a minisub. We didn't think that the Argentine military had any, but we've been wrong about stuff like that before . . .* Surely that was where he and Lukas were, strapped into an Argentine minisub, which was now closing up to encase them in its steel. Lukas, whose face he could just see through the gloom, looked as terrified as Max felt.

Then, one by one, the lights went off.

They were in complete darkness.

Max felt his pulse racing. He forced himself to breathe more slowly and carefully. He had never been so frightened. His ears hurt. His eyes stung. He closed them in an attempt to calm himself. On the edge of his hearing was the sound of the minisub's engines. They were moving. He tried not to think of the water above, below and all around him. He tried not to think of how tiny and insignificant this submarine was in the vast expanse of the South Atlantic Ocean.

And he tried not to think about what awaited him and Lukas.

Max could hear no movement in the darkness. He had no idea what time it was. All he knew was that he was getting colder. Unlike the frogmen, he and Lukas had no wetsuits to keep them warm. The chill started at his extremities then travelled to his core. He shivered: his body was doing everything it could to keep warm. But he also knew that it wouldn't last for long. The cold water was sapping everything from him: warmth, energy, life.

The shivering grew faster. Then, alarmingly, it slowed. His body was shutting down, preserving energy. He began to feel disorientated again, and he knew hypothermia was close. It was an effort even to breathe through the oxygen mouthpiece.

An effort even to panic . . .

A sudden muffled clunk penetrated Max's consciousness. He managed to feel a twinge of fear. A single beam of light shot through the gloom. Then, a couple of seconds later, several more. Figures swam in front of Max's eyes. He felt himself being unclipped from the vessel. The muffled mechanical grind returned and he knew the minisub was opening up. Somebody pulled the oxygen mask from his face and he felt himself being lifted once more by the ankles and the shoulders. Out of the corner of his eye he saw Lukas's face, suddenly very close before it receded again into the gloom. And then he felt himself being manoeuvred out of the vessel.

He could tell he was underwater and in open sea: the currents were strong and swirling. He knew that if his abductors let go of him, he was dead. With his wrists and ankles bound, swimming was impossible and the current would immediately take him. As the burning sensation began to build up in his lungs once more, he felt one of them wrapping something around his waist and between his legs.

Then they let go.

Instinctively, Max started to writhe. He couldn't help it. He was drifting, unsupported. He had to get to the surface. He had to get some air. He couldn't even tell which way was up. He blew a few precious bubbles into the water and watched to see which way they travelled. But no matter how he twisted his body, he couldn't seem to follow them.

He was sinking, fast . . .

Then, from nowhere, a jolt. Whatever his abductors had wrapped around his waist tightened. He felt himself being pulled upwards. There was a sudden splash and a roar as he broke the surface and his hearing returned. He inhaled, gasping noisily as he sucked oxygen back into his system. He couldn't understand what was happening: he was suspended in mid-air, swinging like a pendulum, face-down over the water. The sea receded as he was lifted higher and higher. Then he looked to his left and realised what was happening.

He saw an old fishing trawler. The hull was a dirty grey, the bridge white. A crane stood on the starboard deck. Max was being winched out of the water by the crane, hooked by a carabiner fitted to a waist harness. The ship yawed and rocked. The movement made Max dizzy as he swung towards the vessel, now close to the railings, now far away, and finally directly above the main deck. The winch lowered him and he hit the deck with a painful thump.

Figures surrounded him. They wore dark green life jackets and military helmets. One man unclipped him from the winch and cut the cables that bound his ankles. Another pulled him roughly from the deck. They barked at him and dragged him towards the stern of the boat. Nothing in their voices or body language was friendly. Max was under no illusion that he was a prisoner.

Battered and drained of energy, Max was thrown to the floor by the stern railings, next to an orange lifeboat. Lukas was already there. His wrists were tied behind him to a post that carried a life ring. Max was dragged into position next to him and his wrists were similarly bound. The guys in green life jackets left them with a grunt. As they walked away, a wave crashed over the side of the boat, but Max barely felt it: he could not have been wetter, or colder. The sound of the trawler's engines filled his ears, occasionally punctuated by a rolling boom as a wave hit the hull. He had to shout to be heard. His voice, raw and high-pitched, barely sounded like his own.

'I thought we were going to die!' he yelled.

'There's time yet.'

'Why have they brought us here?'

Another wave crashed over them, and Max felt his stomach slip with the movement of the boat before Lukas could reply.

'To find out who we are and what we know. To question us.' Lukas curled his lip. 'They can question us all they want,' he said. 'I'm not telling them anything.'

Max didn't answer. There was no need for him to articulate what he was thinking: that questioning by these Argentine forces was likely to be brutal and painful. That there was only so long an individual could withstand interrogation under torture.

And when the interrogation was done, what then? Would they be allowed to go home? Hardly. They would surely be killed.

Max glanced out over the ocean. It looked like a vast, watery grave.

12

The Woman in the Window

Lili and Abby had to hold Sami back to stop him wading into the ocean. Sami struggled hard. He was a lot stronger than his wiry frame suggested.

'Sami! Stop it! We're wasting time! The more time we waste, the less chance we have to rescue them, keep them alive!'

Abby's words had an immediate effect. Sami stopped struggling and the two girls let go. But when Sami turned to look at Lili, he had fire in his eyes. '*You* stopped me going to check on them. Now see what's happened!'

Abby was watching Lili as he said this. Her expression changed: anger flooded over it. 'How *dare* you blame me for this? Max and Lukas would have done *exactly* the same thing in our shoes.'

'You don't know that.'

'Yes, I do!'

'*HEY!*' Abby stepped between them, like a referee in a boxing ring. She genuinely thought they might start fighting.

'Exactly what is this achieving? How is this stupid argument helping them? Huh?'

Her two friends fell silent.

'We need to get back to the guest house and alert the Watchers. This is out of our hands now.' Sullenly, Sami and Lili nodded. They were silent, but Abby could still sense the fire between them. 'Come on,' she said.

Never had their fitness been so important. They sprinted back across the beach and up the ridge without slowing down. At the clifftop, they hurtled towards the road at top speed. They were barely out of breath by the time they had run back into Stanley and wound through the streets of the sleepy town to the front door of the guest house. Everything was still and silent. No sign of anyone. They crept back into the guest house. Abby winced when the stairs creaked as they climbed them, and for a few seconds they all froze, listening for evidence that they had disturbed Arlene. They heard none, so they continued upstairs and headed straight into Max's room.

The understanding that Max would be in charge of the sat phone had been unspoken. There were no ranks in the Special Forces Cadets, but the others quietly deferred to him in most matters. That he, along with Lukas, was in great danger, unnerved the three of them. But Abby was honest enough with herself to admit that the desperation she felt in the pit of her stomach went further than concern for a team-mate. She told herself to smother that feeling. But it was difficult, standing here in Max's empty room, the bed still unmade, as though he'd just stepped out of it.

She caught Lili staring at her and strode up to the bed. Max had stowed the suitcase underneath it. She pulled it out, placed it on the mattress and opened it up. The sat phone was in the hidden compartment. She activated it and dialled the number they had all memorised. It only rang a couple of times before Hector answered. If he was surprised at receiving a call at this time of night, he didn't sound it.

Go ahead, Max.

Abby glanced at the others and steeled herself. 'It's Abby,' she said. 'We've got a problem.'

She had to hand it to Hector. During training he could rant and scream at them like a lunatic. But now he was calm and he listened. Abby told him how they'd split up and why. How the frogmen had arrived again, and how she'd seen them digging in a weapons cache. Then she told him about the abduction.

For a moment, Hector was silent. Then he said:

Are you certain Max and Lukas were alive when you saw them?

Abby thought back. She pictured Max's and Lukas draped over the frogmen's shoulders, their faces grainy in the light of the NV binoculars. 'Certain,' she said with confidence. 'They were alive.'

Are you sure you saw those guys caching a Stinger?

'I . . . I think so. I've never seen one in real life, but I'm pretty sure, yes.'

There was a pause. Then Hector said:

We have to get you out of there. Right now.

'What? Why?'

If the frogmen have Max and Lukas alive, they'll be interrogating them. Max and Lukas will give up your position.

'I . . . I don't think they'd do that.'

Trust me, they will. Maybe not immediately, but eventually. They're in for a bad time. As soon as the Argentines learn where you are, they'll send someone in to deal with you. You have to get out of there. Leave all your stuff where it is. Make your way back to the cove, immediately.

'But we've just come from the cove.'

Get back there, now.

'What about Max and Lukas? We can't just leave them . . .'

Right now, we can't do anything else. We don't know where they are.

'B-but as soon as the Argentines have finished questioning them, they'll k-kill them . . .'

There was another pause.

Not on my watch. Get out of there. Now.

The line went dead.

Abby looked at Lili and Sami. Their eyes were wide with dread.

'Well?' Lili whispered.

'We've got to get out,' Abby said.

Max was still achingly cold. He could barely talk. His vision swam in and out of focus. The booming of the waves against the hull of the fishing trawler echoed in his head. His chin dropped to his chest and he was only vaguely aware of Lukas's voice. 'Someone's coming!'

Max lifted his heavy head. He saw two dark figures approaching, now blurry, now sharp. There was a light somewhere behind them. It blinked in and out of sight as they approached. When they stopped, it shone into the space between them, dazzling Max.

'Who are you?' a guttural voice said in English, with a pronounced accent. His face came into view. The whites of his eyes were red. A tattoo covered his left cheek. It was the man who had killed the old farmer. The man who had attacked Max at the listening station. He oozed violence.

'No one,' Max said. 'You've made a mistake. We were just –'

There was no warning. The man hit him suddenly and violently: a brutal punch to the nose. Max felt blood flow from his nose. Then he felt thick fingers around his throat, tight and threatening.

'Who are you?'

Max was so exhausted that for a moment he considered telling them. It would be so much easier, because maybe then they would let him get warm, and sleep. But then the image of his friends' faces swam in his mind. Lili. Sami. And in front of them both, Abby. He felt a surge of defiance. 'We're no one,' he repeated. 'We're just here on holiday. I have no idea what's going on. What have we done?'

He could tell his words had an effect. The man loosened his grip and looked at his companion. They exchanged a few words in their own language. Then the man looked back at Max. 'If you're lying to us . . .'

'We just want to go home,' Max said, in as small a voice as possible.

'You're not going anywhere,' the red-eyed man said, and he gave a harsh bark of a laugh. There was no humour in that laugh. The two men walked away.

Max and Lukas looked at each other. 'You know what that meant?' Lukas said.

'Yeah,' Max said. 'I know what that meant.' He set his jaw. 'We have to hold out as long as possible. We can't let them know about the others . . .'

His chin dropped to his chest again. Blood trickled from his nose.

Abby, Lili and Sami crept back down the stairs, wincing again as they creaked. Hector's urgency had freaked them out. The very walls of the guest house seemed to close in on them. It didn't feel safe.

They stepped out into the street and closed the front door behind them. They crossed the deserted road, ready to run out of Stanley again. Abby glanced back at Atlantic View guest house. It would be the last time she set eyes on it.

Then her heart almost stopped.

The curtains were parted at a first-floor window. A face was at the glass.

It was an old face, pale and ghostly. At first Abby thought it was just that: a ghost. But that was only because she didn't immediately recognise the old woman's face. By day, Arlene was jolly and kind. Now, though, she was glaring at them with suspicion. Her eyes narrowed. She stepped away and out of sight.

'Did you see that?' Abby said.

'See what?' Lili and Sami said in unison.

'Arlene. She was watching us from the window.'

There was silence.

'It's probably nothing,' Sami said.

Typical Sami, Abby thought. So trusting. She shook her head. 'I don't think so. She didn't seem friendly. And remember what Hector said? That there might be Argentine spies on the island?'

'Her?!' Lili whispered.

'Everyone knows Arlene,' Abby hissed, repeating Peter's words. 'Think about it. How come the frogmen knew to find Max and Lukas at the listening station? What if Arlene had been speaking to Peter and found out what happened today? What if she's an Argentine agent and she tipped them off?'

Sami and Lili gave her a horrifed look. 'We need to get going,' Lili said.

There was no further argument. The three cadets sprinted back through the capital towards the road that had now become very familiar to them. They didn't speak. There was nothing to say. Abby was certain that Stanley was not a safe place for them any more. As they sprinted back along the long, straight road, she kept checking back over her shoulder. She had an uncomfortable feeling that somebody was watching them. As she ran, she tried to tell herself that she was just unnerved by the sight of the old woman in the window.

When they were three-quarters of the way along the road, she saw lights.

'Someone's coming!' she shouted.

The others slowed a little and looked back. Their faces said it all. This was the first time they'd seen any vehicle on the road after dark. It didn't bode well.

They carried on running. Abby was eager to get off the road, but that would be counter-productive. To the right was sea. To the left was land, but that direction would take them away from the cove. They had no option but to continue along the coast road until it turned back on itself and they could head cross-country. Every time she checked, however, the headlights were closer.

Could the occupants of the vehicle see them? She didn't know. All she knew was that she was getting tired. They all were – they were slowing down. It was a massive relief when they reached the turn in the road that meant they could go across country. But they'd only been running along the grass for a minute when, behind them, Abby saw the unmistakable beams of three torches lighting up the sky. 'They're following,' she gasped. 'We have to move quicker!'

There had been times, back at Valley House, when she had truly hated the Watchers for beasting them in their fitness sessions. Now she was grateful. Because although her muscles shrieked and her lungs felt as though they would burst and she was desperate to stop and catch her breath, she had felt like this before and knew it was possible to break through it. The three of them did not let up. They raced across the uneven ground towards the cove as Hector had told them to, painfully aware that the people with torches were following them, but not deviating from their course. The cove was getting closer, and although it hardly felt like a safe haven, if it was a choice between that and turning to face whoever was following them, Abby knew which option she favoured.

Finally they saw the clifftop up ahead: the boulders and the copse were silhouetted against the night sky. They veered towards the ridge and, moments later, were hurtling down to the cove. There was no sign of the torches now. They half ran, half stumbled downhill in the darkness and a minute later were on the beach. They could see their own footprints in the sand, and the footprints of others, but they focused on the ocean. Standing at the base of the cliff, so they couldn't be seen from above, they looked out to sea.

And saw nothing.

'We're trapped here,' Lili said breathlessly. 'If those people following us decide to come down the ridge . . .'

'Look!' Abby said, and pointed towards the water.

They were distant and faint at first: two dark smudges on the horizon. They were clearly moving fast though. Within seconds, Abby could see that they were two RIBS – rigid inflatable boats. She thought she could see four passengers in one boat, two in the other.

'Who is it?' Sami asked.

'It's the SBS,' Abby said.

'How can we be sure?' Lili demanded. 'What if it's the Argentines?'

'We know they approach by minisub to avoid being seen,' Abby replied. 'These people don't care about that. They're supposed to be here. It means they're British. Come on, let's get to the water's edge.'

'*Wait!*' Lili whispered. '*Look!*' She was pointing to their right, back towards the ridge. Beams of light were shining from that direction. 'They're coming. What do we do?'

'Stay here,' Sami said. He sounded calm. 'Wait till the boats are close. They'll cover us as we run down to the water.'

'What if they don't even know we're here?' Abby said.

'They know we're here,' Sami said. 'They'll be watching us.' He lifted both hands in the air and waved in the direction of the RIBs, which continued speeding towards them.

Abby stared from the ridge to the RIBs and back again. She was trying to estimate how long they had before the people with the torches arrived at the beach. Less than a minute, certainly. And what of the RIBs? How long till they reached shore? That was harder to gauge. They kept disappearing as the waves rose and fell. Would they get to the water in time? A panicked sensation in her gut said no.

Twenty seconds passed.

Thirty.

The RIBs were twenty metres from the shore.

Their pursuers were almost on the beach.

'*Let's go!*' Abby hissed.

They sprinted. Their instinct was to stay close together, but they resisted it. Bunched up, they presented a single, easy target. Spread out, they would give their pursuers a tougher time of it, if they were armed. They ran at five-metre intervals. As she belted towards the water, Abby looked over at the ridge. Their pursuers had reached the bottom. Their torches were pointing in the cadets' direction. There was shouting . . . then a shot echoed out into the night.

As soon as the shot rang out, one of the RIBs curled off to the ridge end of the beach. It had a general-purpose machine gun mounted at the bow, manned by one of the crew. A burst of automatic fire exploded from the GPMG. In her peripheral vision, Abby saw their pursuers hit the ground and she knew that the shooters in the RIB were laying down suppressing fire to allow the cadets to approach the other vessel. Seconds later they were knee-deep in water and the closest RIB had performed a crash stop, turning 90 degrees to port and presenting the beam of the boat to the beach. There were two other people in the boat. One was at the wheel, the other was gripping the port side of the RIB. Abby couldn't make out their faces, but then one of them shouted at the top of their voice: '*GET IN! NOW!*'

'Angel,' Abby breathed. The RIB was ten metres away. She plunged into the ocean and swam through the waves as powerfully as she could. Thirty seconds later she was clambering over the slippery side of the inflatable boat, the first of the three cadets to do so. She felt a strong arm grip her: Angel, pulling her roughly into the boat. She tumbled in, aware of more suppressing fire in the background. Woody had the wheel, and he wore an expression of grim determination on his normally friendly face. Angel pulled the other two into the boat. '*Go!*'

There was a low roar from the RIB's motor, and a surge. The boat curled around in a tight circle and headed out to sea, ploughing recklessly through the waves. Salt and spray covered the cadets and glowed in the moonlight.

13

HMS *Stirling*

The worst thing was the waiting.

Max and Lukas knew that the red-eyed frogman and his mate would return. And they knew that, when that happened, there would be more violence. Max half wanted to get it over with.

Yeah, waiting was the worst.

The fishing trawler was in motion. Max passed the time trying to determine their direction of travel. It was cloudy. From time to time, though, the clouds parted and he could make out the Southern Cross twinkling in the sky. Each time it came into view, he extended an imaginary line from the top of the cross down its long axis, five times its length, then dropped the line down to the horizon. This told him where south was, but that wasn't much use. The Southern Cross kept disappearing and reappearing with a new bearing. They seemed to be travelling in a circle. But that didn't make sense, did it?

Spray covered them. They were soaking wet, so it was difficult for Max to tell if his nose was still bleeding. He was certainly still in pain, and the pain increased when he saw the two figures approach again. When they were close, he saw that the red-eyed guy held a handgun. The man knelt in front of Max and put the gun to his forehead.

'Who are you?' he rasped over the noise of the engines and the ocean.

Max swallowed hard. 'No one.'

The man nodded and gave a grim smile. Then, without taking his eyes from Max, he aimed the handgun at Lukas instead. His implication was clear: Answer me, or your friend dies.

'Who are you?' he repeated.

Max glanced sidelong at Lukas. His friend was looking straight ahead. He seemed calm, and Max understood why. So long as their captors thought Max and Lukas had information, they were more valuable alive than dead. 'Please don't hurt him,' Max said. 'We're just here on holiday. We don't know what's going on.'

The man's red eyes narrowed. He stood up, turned to his mate and nodded. They moved away along the deck.

The RIB carrying Woody, Angel, Lili, Sami and Abby sped through the waves. Conversation was impossible. The cadets gripped the sides of the RIB. Their clothes were sodden and heavy, their eyes blinded by spray. All Abby saw was dark, threatening sea and endless cloudy sky. They seemed to be speeding into the middle of nowhere. Her eyes fell on

Angel and Woody and it was impossible not to feel slightly reassured. They were like the cadets' parents, siblings and best friends all rolled into one. They schooled them, trained them and comforted them. Woody's friendly face and Angel's fiery red hair were a source of encouragement. They knew what they were doing and would stop at nothing to ensure the cadets' safety.

But there were some things they couldn't do. Like bring people back from the dead. She tried not to think about what had happened to Max and Lukas. Could they possibly still be alive? She shuddered when she thought of what could be happening to them right now.

They had been travelling for perhaps five minutes when a vessel suddenly appeared on the horizon. It looked like a large military ship. Abby remembered Hector telling them that Woody and Angel would be stationed on a Royal Navy patrol ship with a Special Boat Service unit. Surely this was it.

Minutes later they were in the shadow of the enormous steel-grey vessel. Being alongside it somehow made the ocean feel deeper and scarier. There was a deafening engine-grind and the salty air was thick with the stench of fuel oil. The second RIB drew up alongside them and for the first time Abby could see its occupants properly: four armed men in wetsuits and life jackets, one of them still manning the GPMG. The SBS? She reckoned so.

'Stay put!' Angel shouted. For once, Abby resisted making the obvious sarcastic remark. *Do we have to? I fancied a quick swim*. Instead, she gripped the side of the RIB and, following Woody's lead, looked up. A giant crane hovered above them, over the side of the patrol ship. Woody stood up in the boat. A set of ropes with attached carabiners was winched down, and Woody reached out to grab them. He clipped the ropes to anchor points on the RIB, then took a torch from his life jacket and shone it up towards the deck. The RIB rose from the water's surface, buffeted by the wind. Abby's stomach lurched as the RIB was swung over the railings. The winch lowered it down into a metal frame onto the deck. They were aboard.

Abby took a few seconds to take in their surroundings. They were at the stern of the ship. High above them were the vessel's communications masts and air-surveillance radars. Across the deck was a helicopter landing pad. There were crew members dotted around, in black berets and storm coats, all of them seemingly busy. A man was waiting for them. He had greying hair, a full beard and a bearing that told Abby, without her having to ask, that this was the ship's captain. Woody and Angel jumped out of the RIB and strode up to him. 'What do we know?' Woody shouted.

The captain looked from Woody to the three teenagers. His brow was furrowed and he didn't immediately reply. Abby got it. It must have been quite a surprise to see three kids being winched up from the South Atlantic. The existence of the Special Forces Cadets was a secret to almost everybody, this guy included. Abby could see a hundred questions crossing his face. Woody stepped up to him. 'They have full security clearance,' he said. 'You speak to them as you speak to us.'

'On my vessel,' the captain said, 'I speak to anyone as I choose.'

'Would you like us to get London involved?' Woody asked.

A muscle in the captain's right cheek twitched. 'That won't be necessary,' he said. 'Follow me.' He turned on his heel and stalked along the deck towards the bridge.

'What are you waiting for?' Woody asked the cadets.

The cadets jumped out. Their sodden clothes dripped as they followed the captain, Woody and Angel. They drew perplexed glances from the other crew members on deck, which was no surprise to Abby. But nobody stopped them to ask awkward questions. It must have been obvious to them all, from the captain's march along the deck, that serious business was afoot.

They left the deck through a heavy door. The captain led them up some metal stairs and into the main control room of the bridge. Abby stopped beside Angel. 'Where are we?' she asked.

'HMS *Stirling*,' Angel said. 'It's a Royal Navy offshore patrol vessel. Fifty crew members, top speed twenty-four knots, range five thousand nautical miles. Thirty-millimetre automatic cannon, two miniguns, four machine guns and two Pacific 24 seaboats. Welcome aboard.'

'Thanks,' Abby muttered. There was something ominous about the way Angel had made a point of listing the ship's weaponry and firepower. 'Do we know anything about Max and Lukas?'

A shadow crossed Angel's face. 'Not yet,' she said. 'Let's hear what the captain has to say.'

The bridge was light and low-ceilinged. There were six other Royal Navy men in here, sitting at high-backed chairs in front of an impressive array of navigation and communications equipment. The captain walked up to one of the crew members, who was sitting at a large screen displaying nautical charts.

'Show us,' he said.

The man pointed to a blinking dot on the screen. 'This is us,' he said. 'We have a fix on all vessels within a hundred-mile radius. They're mostly private vessels or Argentine fishing boats. Our understanding is that British citizens have been removed from the Falklands in a minisub. If we eliminate all those vessels out of range of these minisubs, we're left with five ships. Four of them are heading back to harbour in the Falklands. Which leaves this one, at a 275-degree bearing from our current position.' He pointed at another blinking dot.

'What is it?' Woody said.

'It's an Argentine fishing trawler. It's been circling in this area for as long as we've been tracking it.'

'How big is it?'

'Eight metres.'

'So big enough to host a military force?'

'Perhaps. There may also be regular submarines in the vicinity. The presence of the minisubs would certainly suggest so.'

'We've been attempting radio contact with the trawler,' the captain said, 'but there's no reply. That's usually a giveaway.'

Woody turned to the captain. 'I'd like to request that we set course to intercept that vessel. We think we have friends on board.'

The captain turned to the crew member. 'Do it,' he said. He looked back at Woody and the others. 'I've assigned you a couple of cabins. There's dry gear in there. Anything you need, let me know.'

'How long before we make the intercept?' Angel said.

'About forty-five minutes.'

'That's too long. Can't we get there any quicker?'

The captain narrowed his eyes, clearly unimpressed with Angel's abrupt questioning. However, it was equally clear that he understood the seriousness of the situation. 'My men will get us there as quickly as they can. Now, if you'll excuse me, I'll need to brief the SBS team. They'll board the trawler when we get close. Their equipment is already aboard the RIBs.' He gave the cadets a meaningful stare. 'Make sure you stay out of their way. They're the professionals, not you.'

The captain's assistant led them from the bridge, back the way they had come and then below decks. The crew's living quarters were off cramped corridors. There was one cabin for the boys and one for the girls. Abby followed Angel and Lili into their cabin and was grateful to find dry towels there. Two sets of clothes waited for each cadet: regular military fatigues, waterproof trousers and storm coats, and a wetsuit and life jacket. The cadets stripped, dried and changed. There was no discussion about which set of clothes to wear. They all put on the wetsuits and life jackets. If there was work to be done, they needed to be properly prepared.

Abby sat on the edge of her bunk. A wave of tiredness

crashed over her. She put her head in her hands, overwhelmed by the seriousness of their situation. Immediately, Angel was by her side, one arm around her shoulders.

'What if they're dead?' Abby said.

'We don't deal in "what ifs",' Angel said, her voice uncharacteristically gentle. 'We deal in facts. The fact is, you saw them take Max and Lukas alive. That gives us hope. And while there's hope, we don't give up. Agreed?'

Abby breathed deeply. 'Agreed,' she said. She stood up. 'I want to be on deck. It doesn't feel right, hiding down here.'

Angel nodded. She opened the door and led Abby and Lili outside. Woody and Sami were exiting their cabin at the same time. Silently they filed along the corridor, up the stairs at the end and onto the deck.

The Watchers led them to the bow. From here, it was clear from the rush of wind in their faces and spray from the prow cutting through the waves that the patrol vessel was making good headway. Abby checked the sky. The clouds had parted and she soon identified the Southern Cross. Seconds later she had established that they were heading in a roughly westerly direction. She gripped the deck railings and closed her eyes. Max's face appeared in front of her, as clear as if he was really there, then Lukas's.

'We're coming,' she whispered. 'We're coming to get you. Whatever it takes.'

When she opened her eyes again, it had started to rain and the others were staring at her. If they thought she was weird, talking to herself like that, they didn't let it show. In fact, they appeared even more determined than before.

14

Pathfinder

'Something's happening.'

Max's head lolled on his chest. He'd given up trying to navigate. His eyes were closed. He felt sick, tired, and in pain, but Lukas's tone of voice made him open his eyes. 'What did you say?'

'Something's happening.'

Lukas was right. There was a renewed burst of activity on the boat. Frogmen were hurrying over to the starboard side. RIBs were being winched down into the ocean. Men were shouting instructions at each other. And was it Max's imagination, or had the trawler's engines stopped? There was less vibration on deck. Less mechanical noise.

Lukas was right. Something was happening.

'I think they're mobilising,' Lukas said. 'I think they're launching an attack.'

Max thought about the transponder back at the listening station. He wished he'd managed to destroy it, but he hadn't.

It meant fast air – incoming aircraft on a bombing mission – could score a direct hit on the station in the event of an attack on the Falklands. He looked up into the night sky. Was that attack imminent? Something told him that it might be.

Figures approached. Max and Lukas's interrogators were returning. Their handguns were holstered across their chests and they carried something much worse than weapons.

Body bags.

The bags were the length of a tall man, fastened with sturdy zips along the top. The interrogators laid them out on the deck. One in front of Max, one in front of Lukas. They said nothing. They just gave Max and Lukas a meaningful glare and walked away again.

'They're trying to scare us into talking,' Lukas said. Something in his voice suggested to Max that he was trying to persuade himself that this was true. 'We need to keep them guessing for as long as possible. The others will be here soon.'

'The others don't know where we are,' Max said. His face was agony. The rest of his body was numb with cold. He could feel his motivation slipping away.

'They'll work it out.'

'You reckon? I can't help thinking of that old farmer last night. They took him out to sea when he was already dead, remember? They must have done that so they could get rid of the body.' He nodded at the body bags. 'You reckon they stuffed him in one of those?'

Lukas didn't have a chance to reply. The two interrogators were approaching again. They were carrying rocks the size of footballs. The rocks were obviously heavy. A strain to carry. The men dropped them next to the body bags, then unzipped the bags and stuffed the rocks inside. When they stood up again, the guy with the red eyes looked at Lukas and Max in turn. He spat at them, then the two men walked away again.

'Maybe we should talk,' Max said.

'If we talk,' Lukas said, 'they'll kill us. No question.'

'Then what do we do?'

'We wait,' Lukas said. 'The others *will* be here soon.'

Max said nothing.

'How long?' Abby said.

She was still standing at the bow of the ship, rain lashing against her face. Sami and Lili were on one side of her, Angel and Woody on the other. It was difficult, somehow, surrounded only by water and sky, to keep track of time.

But before anybody could answer, there was a sudden change in the sound of the patrol ship's engines. Abby sensed a shift in the vessel's momentum. They were changing course.

'What's happening?' Sami said.

They turned back towards the bridge. The captain was striding in their direction. Abby could instantly tell, from his expression, that something was wrong. Panic rose in her gut. She stepped forward, but Angel put one hand on her arm to restrain her.

'What is it?' Woody said.

'We have new orders from London,' the captain said. 'Follow me.'

'Wait!' Sami shouted. 'What's going on? We need to intercept that fishing trawler!'

The captain didn't answer. He had already turned his back on them and was heading back along the deck. 'Do what he says,' Angel told them. Her voice was tense. Her eyes flashed. 'Let's go.'

They were silent as the captain led them back onto the bridge. It was immediately clear that something important had happened. There were more people in here now. At least fifteen men. Some were scrutinising the navigation screens. Others were typing furiously on keyboards. There was a general hubbub of radio noise. Three men were speaking urgently over the ship's comms system.

'What's happening?' Woody demanded.

'We've detected suspicious movement of vessels originating from the trawler,' the captain said.

'Then we need to get there as soon as we can!' Abby told him.

'It's not as simple as that, young lady. There are other factors at play here.'

'Our friends are on that boat!'

'That may be, but we have a bigger problem.'

'Bigger than –' Abby started to say, but a look from Angel silenced her.

'There is a sizeable movement of personnel from the trawler towards the Falkland Islands. We're talking multiple RIBs, and sonar is picking up a number of submersibles.'

'How many vessels?' Woody asked.

'Hard to say. Twenty, maybe more. A Pathfinder force in

all likelihood. The Argentines are launching an attack. It's happening. Now. I'm sorry, our priorities have changed. If the Argentine troops make land, the lives of everyone on the Falkland Islands are at risk. We're the only naval vessel in the vicinity. We have to cut them off. We don't have any choice.'

'*No!*' Abby whispered. 'Max and Lukas . . . You can't leave them –'

'I have no choice, young lady. I have to balance the lives of two military personnel with the lives of everyone in Stanley and beyond.'

'But they're our friends!' Lili and Sami shouted in unison.

A grim expression fell across the captain's face. 'And what difference do you think that makes?' he said. 'You think we make decisions based on what is best for our friends, rather than what is for the greater good?' His eyes narrowed again. 'I don't know who you kids are or why you're here. I've got a feeling I'll never find out. But if you think you're going to make it in the military, you'd better understand this: sometimes we have to make tough choices. This isn't the playground; this is the real world.' He addressed Woody and Angel. 'I want these children off the bridge and below decks. They're not to leave their quarters until I give the word. I'm holding you responsible for them.'

Neither Woody nor Angel replied. They simply inclined their heads politely. The captain turned his back on them and started to bark orders at his men.

'This way,' Angel said quietly, and she led them from the bridge.

None of the cadets spoke until they were alone at the top of the stairwell. 'You didn't even argue with him!' Abby hissed, accusation dripping from her voice.

'Did he look to you like a man who was going to change his mind?'

'Well, no, but . . .'

'We choose our battles wisely, Abby.'

'But Max and Lukas,' Abby snapped back. 'What are we going to do about them?'

Something seemed to pass between Woody and Angel. 'It's too dangerous,' Woody said.

'Do you have a better idea?' Angel said.

'No. But it's too dangerous. You know it is. We're already two cadets down.'

'Not necessarily.'

'Hey, do we get a say in this?' Abby cut in.

There was a moment of silence. 'There's no easy way of getting to Max and Lukas,' Woody said.

'You think we don't know that?'

'Your chances of success are vanishingly small,' Angel added.

'If Max and Lukas were here,' Abby said, 'and two of us were on that trawler, they wouldn't hesitate.'

'That doesn't make it the safe thing to do,' Woody said.

Something flipped inside Abby. 'The safe thing to do?' she hissed. 'We're teenagers. You've sent us in to armed sieges. You've sent us to North Korea. You've sent us into the jungle and into the favelas. Since when did we make decisions based on whether it's the *safe* thing to do?'

'Those risks were calculated,' Woody snapped back. 'Right now, our only way of getting to Max and Lukas is by launching a RIB from this patrol ship and approaching by stealth. It'll take two of us to launch the RIB and that will have to be me and Angel, because we're the only ones with the authority to stop the captain despatching a team to cut you off when he realises what you've done.'

'We're doing it,' Abby said. She looked at Lili and Sami. 'Right?'

'Right,' they agreed.

They were at the foot of the stairs. Angel turned to Woody. 'They grow up fast, huh?' she said.

Woody's friendly face was shrouded in anxiety. He glanced back up the stairwell. 'I don't like it,' he said. 'If they get into trouble on the water, we'll have no way of helping them. It's not a swimming pool out there. It's the South Atlantic and there's a storm coming in.'

'I think they know that, Woody. They're fit and they're capable. They've as much chance of pulling this off as anyone. But we need to move fast.' Angel opened a door that led outside. A violent blast of wind tore through it. 'Are you prepared to do what it takes?' she asked the cadets.

The three cadets looked at each other. Then at the Watchers. Then they nodded.

Woody and Angel led them out onto the aft deck. There were several members of the ship's personnel here, going about their business. None of them paid the cadets any attention. Instinctively, Abby checked for CCTV cameras. She noticed the others doing the same. There were a couple of cameras pointing towards the stern of the ship. The cadets skirted behind them, out of their field of view, and along the starboard deck. The crane was unmanned, but they were not entirely out of view of the sailors on the aft deck. The RIB that had transported them from the cove was on its metal frame, still attached to the ropes by carabiners fastened to three anchor points. The outboard motor was hinged up at a 30-degree angle from the transom at the back of the boat.

'The RIB has a full store of SBS boarding gear,' Angel told them. 'You know what to do with it?'

The cadets nodded. They'd learned the theory, at least, back in Valley House. None of them mentioned the obvious problem: learning a technique in class was one thing, but doing it in practice was quite another.

'You need to head west,' Angel said. 'You can do that? We don't have time to teach you how to use the on-board GPS.'

Abby pointed upwards. 'There's a compass,' she said. 'We can use it to navigate.'

'There's a handheld VHF radio on the RIB. Keep it with you. If you get into trouble, broadcast a distress signal on emergency channel 16. I can't promise it'll do any good, but . . .' Her voice trailed off.

'You should see the trawler's lights within ten minutes if you're heading in the right direction,' Woody said. 'If possible, approach the trawler from the stern. They might be on high alert, but they're less likely to see an infiltration from that direction.'

Angel looked out across the ocean. 'The invasion is out of your hands now. Leave that to the Navy and the Air Force.

You need to concentrate on Max and Lukas. It's going to be dangerous on that trawler. Do whatever it takes to make them safe.'

'Wish us luck,' Abby said.

Angel shook her head. 'No,' she said. 'Luck won't come into it. Make good choices. Stay alert. Look out for each other.' Along the deck a few crew members were still visible. 'We're going to need a distraction before we winch you in,' she said.

'Leave that to me,' Woody said. 'As soon as you see them running, launch the RIB.' He nodded reassuringly at the cadets. Then, without another word, he jogged through the driving rain, along the deck and out of sight.

'What's he going to do?' Abby asked.

'I guess we're about to find out,' Angel replied.

15

RIB

Woody ran up the metal staircase that led to the bridge.

There, the atmosphere was tense. The captain was at his station in the middle of the bridge. His crew were scrutinising on-screen nautical charts and GPS positions. There was a constant background thrum of radio comms. The face of every man on the bridge was creased into intense concentration. None of them even seemed to notice Woody's arrival, until he was standing right by the captain.

The captain blinked heavily. 'I said I wanted you below decks,' he said.

'Lucky for you I had other ideas,' Woody replied.

'What are you talking about?'

'I've just been on the starboard deck. I saw the conning tower of a submarine. It's close. Two hundred metres.'

The captain frowned. 'What are you talking about? If a sub was that close, we'd know about it.'

'I know what I saw,' Woody said. 'I've been on enough

ships and seen enough submarines. You're under surveillance. Possibly under attack.'

A flicker of indecision crossed the captain's face. But it was just that. A flicker. 'All hands to starboard deck!' he shouted across the bridge. 'Now!'

He was facing away from Woody as he said it, so he didn't see the brief smile that crossed Woody's face.

On deck, a horn sounded. Five short blasts, but they were loud enough to make Abby's bones tremble. Then a male voice came over the tannoy. 'All hands to starboard deck. Repeat, all hands to starboard deck.'

The crew members' response was immediate. They ran from their port-side positions and in seconds they were out of sight.

'Get in the RIB!' Angel instructed. 'Fast!'

Abby, Lili and Sami did as they were told, jumping over the inflatable sides of the boat. Angel took up position at the crane's control panel. As soon as the cadets were aboard, she yanked a lever. The slack ropes connecting the RIB to the winch went taut. There was a jolt. Slowly, the RIB rose into the air. Abby felt her stomach drop. She gripped the side of the RIB even more firmly as they rose above the deck railings and swung out over the ocean. The RIB rocked precariously in the wind, and Abby saw her friends' faces etched with concentration and fear. The winch started to lower them towards the ocean. Abby looked over at Angel, who was watching them intently. But as the RIB descended she went out of sight. All they could see was the grey hull of the patrol vessel to one side and the wide open expanse of ocean to the other.

Then, with another jolt, the RIB slapped against the surface of the ocean. Still attached to the winch, it cut through the sea, dragged along by the larger vessel. The cadets scrambled to reach the three anchor points.

'Ready?' Abby screamed above the deafening noise of the patrol vessel's engines. 'In three . . . two . . . one . . . release!'

She unclipped her carabiner and let it go. The RIB swivelled dramatically on its axis – clearly Sami and Lili had not unclipped at quite the same moment. Then there was another jolt and she saw the halyard swing away ahead of the RIB. They were free.

But not safe. The patrol ship was moving ahead of them. Its wash was ferocious. The RIB rose awkwardly on a sudden swell before a powerful wave crashed over it. For a moment, Abby thought she'd been knocked overboard, but then she realised she was on her back in the bottom of the RIB. Sami grabbed her hand and pulled her up while Lili started the RIB's motor. They were clear of the wake now. As Abby looked towards the ship she could just make out Angel, standing at the stern, one arm raised. Abby raised her own arm as Sami took the wheel of the RIB. Moments later they were curling away in a wide circle and heading away from the patrol vessel.

The RIB bounced and planed over the waves. Sami gripped the steering wheel with both hands, watching the sea but also glancing occasionally at the compass in front of the wheel. Abby and Lili busied themselves with locating the gear they were going to require. A telescopic painter's pole with a curved grappling hook was clipped to the interior of the RIB. There was a storage compartment around the steering column where they found coils of strong rope and a rope ladder bundled into a neat cylinder. Abby also located the handheld VHF radio. It had a clip on the back which allowed her to attach it to her life jacket. She kept the radio switched off because she had no desire to hear the commands that were doubtless being issued right now over the airways. There were no firearms, but there were three emergency flares, a set of binoculars and a black-handled knife in a sturdy holster.

'There!' Sami shouted, raising a hand and pointing straight ahead. Abby brushed spray from her eyes and squinted. Through the driving rain she could dimly see some lights on the horizon. They disappeared as the RIB moved from the crest of a wave into a trough, then reappeared, a little clearer this time. The patrol vessel was already out of sight. Anxiety crawled over her skin as she realised how tiny their boat was compared to the vastness of the ocean, and how challenging the task that lay ahead.

But then she thought of Max and Lukas and her anxiety faded away, replaced by a steely determination. 'Keep going!' she shouted. She gripped the side of the boat again and didn't take her eyes from the target.

'Max! They're coming back!'

Max jerked his head up and opened his eyes. Lukas was right. Two indistinct figures were approaching. He saw the two body bags lying on the deck next to them. Then he looked back up. Their two interrogators were standing over them, their expressions cold. Max observed that their handguns were still stowed in their shoulder holsters, which gave him a momentary boost. 'Please . . .' he whispered. 'We're just –'

He was cut short when the red-eyed guy removed a broad-bladed knife from his ops waistcoat. He knelt down in front of Max and stabbed the blade at Max's face. Max flinched. 'Please . . .' he whispered again.

His interrogator muttered something Max didn't understand, then he moved behind Max and Lukas and, with two swift slices, cut the ties that bound their wrists to the post. The relief was immense, but short-lived. The other interrogator grabbed them by the hair and pushed them onto their fronts. Max felt his wrists being seized again. He tried to struggle, but was too weak to be effective. In just a few seconds, his wrists had been retied. His right cheek was pressed against the wet deck. Lukas lay near him. The two interrogators stood at either end of Lukas's body. They bent down. One took his ankles, the other his shoulders. Lukas started to wriggle and shout, but they were too strong for him. They carried him over to one of the body bags and laid him along it, over the open zip. Lukas's struggling became more desperate but, with his arms and ankles bound, there was nothing he could do. One of the men forced his boot onto Lukas's chest, keeping him pinned down. The other knelt down and opened the body bag, pulling it around Lukas's body and forcing him inside.

'Get off me! *Get off me!*' Lukas yelled. His voice became muffled as the man covered his face with one large hand and forced Lukas's head into the body bag.

It was difficult for them to zip it up. Lukas writhed and wriggled. But there were two of them and only one of him. There could only be one outcome. The zip buzzed ominously as they closed up the body bag with Lukas inside. Once it was fully shut, the writhing stopped. There was just a gentle rising and falling, as though Lukas was breathing deeply in an attempt to keep calm.

Then they turned to Max.

The urge to struggle was almost overwhelming. Somehow, though, Max managed to overcome it. His energy reserves were seriously depleted. He needed to conserve as much strength as possible. He told himself that the men were just being threatening. It was a difficult thought to hold on to as they lifted him into the remaining body bag. The rocks they had used to weigh it down poked uncomfortably against the back of his knees, and the body bag itself smelled unpleasantly damp. Max felt a boot against his ribcage and a hand pressed down on his face. The zip closed over his head and he was instantly overwhelmed by panic. He had to concentrate hard on keeping calm.

It wasn't easy.

The body bag was zipped shut. He heard the man saying, 'I'm looking forward to killing you.' The thick plastic lay over his face, and he felt his breath condensing against it. He could hear his heart pounding. It was hard to breathe and he felt his limbs twitching of their own accord. He squeezed his eyes shut, hoping against hope that he was not about to feel himself being lifted again.

Because that could only mean one thing.

There was no movement. Whether the interrogators were still watching them, or whether they had walked away, Max couldn't tell.

Breathe, he told himself.

Breathe . . .

They're coming. They'll be here.

They'll be here soon . . .

Distance to the trawler: three hundred metres.

It seemed to Abby that Sami was steering the RIB like a pro. Their only experience of motor boats had been on the flat waters of the lake at Valley House, and this treacherous sea could not be more different. Their Syrian friend clearly had a talent. As planned, he approached the trawler from behind. The wake of the vessel was substantial, even from a distance. It became stronger the closer they got.

'Are we sure this is the best plan?' Lili shouted as the water became more turbulent. 'It's going to be difficult to operate once we're very close.'

'It's our only option,' Sami shouted back. 'We're least likely to be noticed if we approach from the rear.'

'We need to get the ropes ready,' Abby called. She crawled to the storage area and examined the coils of rope. There were various lengths – short and very long. She took one of the shorter coils and, gripping it firmly, headed to the bow of the RIB. There was an anchoring point at the very front. She took one end of the rope and tied it through the anchoring point. The wet rope burned her palms, but by the time they were within a hundred metres of the trawler it was firmly attached.

They could smell the trawler now. A dirty, oily stench. It overwhelmed the tang of the sea salt. The wake was a torrent and the spray stung their eyes. Sami wore an expression of grim determination as he forced the RIB through the turbulent water. Lili had taken the binoculars and was holding them to her eyes, checking that they weren't being watched from the stern of the trawler. Abby kept her position at the bow, gripping the other end of the rope as they made their final approach.

They were twenty metres from the trawler now. It towered ominously above them.

Ten metres. They juddered through the trawler's wake, the RIB bouncing and jolting. Abby scanned the hull, searching for a fixed point. She located a mooring ring in a roughly central position. She pointed at it and shouted: 'Head for that!' She couldn't even hear her own voice over the noise of the trawler, but Sami followed the line of her finger and manoeuvred the RIB towards the ring. Abby leaned forward from the bow of the boat, one arm outstretched, the other clutching the leading end of the rope. Her fingers struggled for the mooring ring, but it kept slipping out of reach. She leaned out a little further, stretching as far as she could, aware that Lili was by her side, ready to catch her if she leaned too far. She thought of the underwater propellers that were surely just beneath them. They would make short work of a human body . . . Quickly, she put that thought from her mind and leaned forward just a little more . . .

Finally she caught the mooring ring and deftly threaded the rope through it, yanking the leading end up to her chest as she fell back into the RIB. The little boat slammed up against the back of the trawler and Sami fell back from his position at the wheel. He scrambled to his feet and killed the outboard motor while Abby and Lili worked together to hold the rope and tie the free end to the anchoring point at the bow of the RIB. Abby's palms were bleeding and sore from the rope work but at least they were now firmly attached to the trawler. The RIB was surprisingly stable and the wake was less violent this close to the hull.

But that was scant comfort. Kneeling in the RIB, the three cadets looked up. The hull of the boat loomed threateningly over them, faintly illuminated by the white glow of a stern light somewhere out of sight.

Now the three cadets faced their greatest challenge: to climb the hull and board the trawler. They had to hijack this massive vessel and steal back their friends from under the noses of the Argentine special forces.

Assuming, that was, that their friends were still alive . . .

16

Hijack

Breathe . . .

Breathe . . .

The air inside the body bag was thin. Sweat and condensation prickled on Max's salty, bloody face. His chest was tight and he felt sick. He didn't know how much time had passed since he had been zipped into the bag.

Then the zip of the body bag opened. Max sucked in fresh air as rain pelted his face. The red-eyed guy looked down, a snarl on his lips. 'I'm going to give you one more chance to tell me who you are. If you don't, we'll kill you, then throw you overboard. You have ten minutes to think about it.'

'Please . . .' Max whispered.

But the man was already zipping up the body bag. Max was plunged back into darkness.

He believed the threat. Ten minutes. He shivered with fear, then concentrated again on his breathing.

Abby snatched the telescopic painter's pole that was clipped to the side of the RIB. Lili retrieved the rolled-up ladder from the storage area. The ladder had a grappling hook at one end. Abby fitted the painter's pole to the hook then stood at the bow of the boat. She started to extend the pole, length by length. The ladder unfurled as she did so. The uprights of the ladder were made of thick, sturdy wire. The rungs were also wire, but were covered with metal tubing to give them more strength. Abby did her best to hold the telescopic pole stable as she extended it to five metres – not easy on an unstable RIB being dragged roughly through the ocean by a trawler. Lili helped her hold it as it extended to ten metres, then fifteen. The pole banged against the hull of the ship and the ladder flapped and danced in the wind.

By the time the pole had reached the deck railings high above, it took all three of them to hold it steady. They had to move to the back of the RIB to see what they were doing, and that small manoeuvre was also a challenge. Abby's muscles burned as they tried to fit the grappling hook over the lower railings. It took a long, frustrating minute before they eventually managed it. Lili grabbed one of the lower rungs of the ladder and tugged hard to check it was securely attached, then she led it to the bow of the RIB, looked over her shoulders, nodded at Abby and Sami, and began to climb.

Abby could barely watch. The motion of the trawler and the buffeting of the wind meant that the ladder rocked and swung. One moment Lili would be suspended in mid-air, the next her body would be slammed against the ship's hull. She climbed slowly and carefully, only allowing herself to climb a rung when the ladder was relatively still and secure. At no point did she look down. Abby found herself holding her breath as her friend rose higher and higher and, eventually, disappeared over the ship's railings.

Abby turned to Sami and mouthed, over the noise: 'You go next!'

Sami appeared reluctant to let Abby remain alone on the RIB, but she had already started to check the longer coils of rope. They were heavy and bulky. She removed all three and uncoiled them a little. Knot work was second nature to her, thanks to the Watchers' insistence back at Valley House that they practise it blindfolded and for hours at a time. At the time, it had seemed like overkill. Now she was grateful. She decided to use a square knot to securely join the lengths of rope into one super-long length – one hundred and fifty metres long, she estimated – as Sami edged past her and held the ladder. He was lithe and strong and climbed faster than Lili had, perhaps encouraged by having seen her go first. He was over the railings in under a minute.

Which left Abby, alone in the RIB. She had one job to do before climbing the ladder.

Right now, anyone looking over the deck railings would see the ladder and the RIB, and they would know that the trawler had been boarded. They could deal with the ladder once Abby was aboard. The RIB was more problematic. That was where this length of rope would come in. At night, and in these weather conditions, if the RIB trailed the ship by more than a hundred metres it would be invisible to a casual observer on deck. A good plan in theory, but in practice . . .

Abby tied one end of her long rope to one of the free anchoring points at the back of the RIB. She tugged it to make sure it was fast, then located the other end and wrapped it once around her waist and then across her chest. She retrieved the knife from the storage area and stowed it in a pocket. The VHF radio was still clipped to her life jacket. Then she turned to face the ladder.

She was going to have to be quick. Quicker than the others, if she wanted to survive.

She grabbed a rung of the ladder and pulled herself up onto it. Holding on with one hand, she grabbed the knife and awkwardly pulled off the scabbard. Holding the scabbard between her teeth, she leaned down to where the RIB was tied to the trawler. 'Here goes nothing,' she muttered to herself, and put the sharp edge of the knife to the short rope connecting the two vessels. Then she cut it.

The effect was immediate. The RIB, released from the trawler, shot backwards as the trawler forged on through the ocean. It was moving faster than Abby expected – and now she was against the clock. If she didn't reach the deck before the rope went taut, there was every chance that she would be pulled off the rope and into the sea. She reckoned she had twenty seconds, if that.

She sheathed her knife, stowed it again and climbed, groping furiously for the rungs with her hands and feet. They were wet and slippery and it was a struggle to grip them, especially as her palms were still sore from rope burn.

Her stomach lurched with the movement of the trawler, and she had to force herself not to look down . . .

She was halfway up when it happened. The trawler rolled and she found herself suspended from the ladder, hanging in mid-air and swinging towards the sea. She might have screamed – not that she or anyone else would have heard it. What was happening? For an awful moment she thought she had fallen. No, she was still gripping the ladder as her body slammed against the water . . .

Suddenly, she was under. She held on to the ladder with all her might as the trawler, moving relentlessly forward, dragged her through the water. Then she was in the open air again. She saw to her dismay that the handheld VHF radio had become unclipped when she was under the water, but she didn't dare loosen her grip on the ladder. The radio fell from her life jacket into the ocean. Seconds later, she slammed against the hull and the air was knocked from her lungs. Dazed and numb, she forced herself to keep climbing. She couldn't stop for a second . . .

Five metres to go. She could see Sami's face above her, urgent and full of concern. He was reaching out for her, but she still had a quarter of the ladder to climb. She continued to scramble up, rung by rung, her muscles burning, her cold, wet hands gripping the metal tubing as hard as possible . . .

And then she was there, alongside the railings. Sami and Lili hauled her on board. She collapsed onto the deck, soaking and breathless. But she knew she couldn't take a single moment to relax. She uncoiled the rope from around her chest and waist and twisted the free end around the bottom railing and into a reef knot. She had barely finished tying it when the rope became taut. It strained against the knot, but the lashing held fast.

Abby jumped to her feet and looked around. They'd been lucky. There was nobody on the stern deck. It was a cramped area with a couple of old cargo containers, one yellow, one blue, and some buoyancy rings tied to posts.

'Hurry up!' Sami hissed and pointed towards the yellow cargo container. The three cadets sprinted to its far end, where they squeezed out of sight between the container and an adjacent wall. Abby noticed that the door to the container had an external lock and chain, but the lock was undone. She wondered what was inside.

'I thought you'd fallen,' Sami whispered.

'I'm okay,' Abby said, still shaken. 'We need to find Max and Lukas. We can't wait.'

'Quiet!' Lili hissed. 'Someone's coming!'

From their hiding place, Abby could just see two men walk around from the starboard side. They stopped by the cargo container, just out of sight of the cadets. But Abby knew they were still there. She could smell cigarette smoke and then, a few seconds later, could hear them talking in Spanish. She recognised one of the voices: it was the man with the red eyes. Abby had no great skill at languages but Lili was the opposite. Abby couldn't even remember how many languages her friend spoke. Right now, she had her head cocked, listening carefully. As the two men spoke, Lili's eyes widened and she silently seized Abby's arm, as though for reassurance. One of the men laughed unpleasantly. Abby saw a half-smoked cigarette butt on the ground a few metres from where they were hiding. Then the men fell silent.

'What did he say?' Abby whispered.

Lili swallowed hard. 'One of them said, "We'll give them one more chance to tell us who they really are." Then the other one said, "We don't have any more time to waste on the British boys. Let's deal with them now."'

Abby and Sami stared at her. 'We need to get going,' she said.

The zip of the body bag opened. Max inhaled sharply. Rain fell on his face, strangely refreshing. But there was nothing refreshing about the sight of the man who loomed over him.

There was something different in his interrogator's expression – a flatness to his red eyes. He didn't say anything. To Max's left, Lukas lay in his own body bag, the other man leaning over him.

Max's guy had his knife. He held it up to Max's right eye. 'You want to know a secret?' he said.

'What?' Max's throat hurt and his voice was hoarse.

'I'm pleased you haven't told us who you are. Because it means I can do what I wanted to do from the beginning.' The knife blade traced a path down Max's cheek. 'Don't worry. You'll be dead before we throw you over. You won't feel the water seeping into your body bag. You won't feel the sharks ripping through the plastic. But this?' He nodded to indicate the knife. 'This you will feel. This you will *really* feel. So I'm going to give you one last chance: tell me who you are, and what you were doing at the listening station!'

Max drew another long breath to calm himself. Then he said: 'I've got a secret too.'

The interrogator licked his lips. 'What?'

'First,' Max said, 'you have to remove the knife from my eye.'

'The knife stays where it is.'

'Fine,' Max said. 'Then my secret sinks to the bottom of the South Atlantic with me.'

The man hesitated, then withdrew his knife. 'Go ahead,' he said.

'Okay,' Max said. He kept his voice very low, so that the guy had to strain to listen. 'My secret is that I'll be out of this body bag in about twenty seconds.' He waited. Confusion crossed the guy's face. Max nodded over his shoulder.

There, knife in hand, expression grim, stood Abby.

Abby smiled. 'Top of the morning to you.'

And then she attacked.

17

Fight to Win

Make no mistake, Hector had once told them, *fights are not like they appear in the movies. They're short, they're sharp and they're ugly. They open you up to the potential of being mortally wounded or killed outright. Always avoid them if you can. But if you can't, fight to win.*

Abby grabbed the interrogator's knife wrist with one hand and crooked her other arm around his neck. Max, who knew that fighting was a numbers game and that Abby couldn't hope to overcome the man on her own, summoned all his strength. He clenched his stomach muscles and, as suddenly and sharply as possible, sat up. His wrists were still bound behind his back, his ankles were still tied, but he still had a means of attack. He slammed his forehead hard against his interrogator's nose. It wasn't a manoeuvre he would normally attempt, because he risked a broken bone in his own face. But his options were limited. There was a crack and a scream of pain. The guy dropped his knife, which clattered on the metal deck. Max slammed his face into his adversary's nose for a second time. He yelled again. Abby dragged him away from Max, giving Max the opportunity to look over at Lukas.

His friend seemed to have had the same idea. Sami was dragging the other man away from Lukas. Lili had picked up his knife. She slashed the cable ties binding Lukas's wrists and ankles, then strode over to Max and released him.

'You took your time,' Max croaked.

'Sorry about that,' Lili said. She headed over to their two captives and removed the handguns from their shoulder holsters. 'Slight disagreement with the captain of a naval patrol ship. Can you stand?'

Max nodded and shakily stood up. He saw that Abby and Sami still had their guys in neck locks. 'We need to put them somewhere,' he said urgently.

'There are cargo containers at the stern,' Lili said, handing Max a handgun. 'One of them's open, but we can secure it from the outside.'

Max nodded. 'Let's do it.' He took a step forward, and had to grab hold of Lili as he felt his balance going.

'You okay?' Lili said.

'Yeah,' Max whispered. 'But it's been kind of a long night.'

'You could say that.' She bent down and handed Max the red-eyed guy's knife, then gestured with her own knife that Lukas's attacker should stand up. The guy couldn't speak because Sami's neck lock was too tight. He gave Max a stare of such hatred, however, that Max was in no doubt that if he wriggled free, he would attack immediately.

'Move,' Max said.

They were no more than fifteen metres from the stern of the trawler. The area was strangely deserted. This bothered Max, but he needed to focus on helping the others. They shuffled their captives along the deck and to the stern. Here, Max saw the cargo containers the other cadets had mentioned, one yellow, one blue. They forced the two guys to the back of the yellow cargo container, where there was a door with an open padlock. Lili removed the padlock and opened the door. Abby and Sami shoved the two men inside and Lili slammed the door shut then locked the padlock. She stood with her back to the container and allowed herself a smile. 'For a minute there,' she said, 'I thought maybe this wasn't such a good idea.'

'We need to get off the ship.' Sami pointed to the stern. 'We're towing the RIB. We need to haul it in . . .'

'No,' Max interrupted him. 'Something's not right.'

'Max,' Lukas said, 'we *really* need to get off this boat.'

Max turned to Lili. 'You said you had a disagreement with the captain of a naval patrol ship. Why?'

Lili blinked at him. 'They were coming to intercept the trawler,' she said. 'But then they detected vessels heading back towards the Falklands. They think it's a Pathfinder force and that the invasion's going to be tonight. And we don't want to get caught up in that, do we?'

The others shook their heads – all apart from Max. 'When we were on deck, before they put us in the body bags, it looked like there was an attack force mobilising,' he said.

'So what's the problem?' Lili asked. 'What you saw confirms what the patrol ship detected.'

'Yeah, but check out this ship.' He raised one arm to indicate the trawler. 'You really think they're going to launch a major attack from a vessel like this? I don't think they had more than twenty RIBs on the whole thing.'

'How can you be sure?' Lili said. 'I'm guessing they didn't give you a guided tour when they brought you aboard.'

'No,' Max agreed. 'They certainly didn't. But the deck's deserted, apart from those two.' He pointed at the cargo container. 'Does this look like the centre of operations for a full-blown attack on the Falklands?'

'He's right,' Abby said. 'Compare it to HMS *Stirling*. It's a heap.'

'What if the Pathfinder force that the *Stirling* detected is a decoy?' Max said. 'What if it's drawing British forces *away* from the real attack force . . .'

The cadets stared at each other. 'The Stinger,' Abby said. 'If they can lure aircraft from the RAF base away from their real landing spot, they can land on the island, arm themselves with surface-to-air missiles – and then take out whatever aircraft they need to!'

'We need to warn them,' Lukas said. 'Did you bring a VHF radio? We can broadcast on the emergency channel.'

'Er . . .' Abby said. 'Slight problem there.'

'Don't tell me you lost it.'

'Yes, Lukas, I lost it when I was hanging from a rope ladder, trying to board this ship to rescue you. Want to make a thing about it?'

'Stop it,' Sami said. His eyes burned. A roll of thunder echoed in the distance, and the rain suddenly grew stronger. 'If Max is right, and we're the only people who've worked this out, we need to discover where the *real* invasion is going to happen.'

'How are we going to do that?' Lili said.

There was a moment of silence. The cadets looked at the cargo container.

'There's no point asking them,' Max said. 'We'll have no way of knowing if they're telling us the truth. We need to find the operations room on this ship. It's the only way we'll find out for sure where the Argentines are truly intending to attack.'

'That means taking the bridge,' Lukas said. 'We know there are armed men on board. We can't do it without weapons.' He looked fiercely at the two handguns they had confiscated from the interrogators.

'If we can find out where the real attack is happening,' Lili said, 'we can try to contact HMS *Stirling* on the ship's radio.'

'Right,' Max agreed. 'But first, we've got a hijacking to finish off.'

'What's the plan?' Sami said. 'We don't know how many crew members are on board. We don't even know how to get to the bridge.'

Max narrowed his eyes. 'We split up,' he said. 'One group advances along the port deck, the other along the starboard. That way, if one group encounters enemy personnel, the other group still has a chance.'

'What if we all get caught?' Sami said.

'Then we fight,' Max said. 'We have no other option. We have to get to the bridge. Lukas, Sami, Lili, you take the port side. Abby and I will take the starboard. One weapon per group. When we get to the bridge, we need to make sure the men on board believe that we're prepared to use our firearms. You all comfortable with that?'

The others nodded. Max checked his handgun, then cocked it and locked it. Lili did the same with hers. Without another word, they split up.

Max and Abby crept to the starboard edge of the stern deck. They stood with their backs to the bulkhead before turning to the starboard deck itself. 'Not going to lie,' Abby whispered, 'your face is a bit of a mess.'

'The guy in the cargo container saw to that,' Max said. His nose and lips were throbbing badly.

'If I didn't know you were as handsome as you are . . .' she started to say, then interrupted herself with a rueful laugh. 'Maybe I'll leave the flirting till later.'

Max allowed himself a smile. 'Yeah,' he said. 'Kind of got other things on my –'

It was Max's turn not to finish his sentence. Abby pressed her lips against his and gave him a lingering kiss. It hurt, but he didn't mind. She was almost business-like as she pulled away. 'There,' she said. 'That's that out of the way.'

'Er, yeah,' Max said. His knees were suddenly weak. 'Er . . .'

'Come on,' Abby said. 'We going to finish this job or what?'

Max nodded. 'Hey, Abby. Thanks for coming to rescue us.'

'Ah, we didn't have much else on,' Abby said. 'Anyway, you're not rescued yet. We're still on board an enemy ship, in case you hadn't noticed. You coming?'

'Roger that,' Max said. And together, with Max clutching his firearm two-handed in the firing position, they turned the corner and faced down the starboard deck.

The deck was in shadow. Visibility was poor in the driving rain. But so far as they could tell, it was all clear. Max and Abby advanced, he slightly ahead of her, weapon raised. The ship listed and they lost their footing, but they managed to remain standing as they moved towards the bow.

Ten metres.

Twenty metres.

They stopped, suddenly. There were two figures straight ahead, grey and indistinct. Max and Abby pressed their backs against the bulkhead again. They waited.

Twenty seconds.

Thirty.

The grey figures faded. Max and Abby continued advancing. There was a brutal crack of thunder somewhere in the distance and the rain fell sideways, pressing them into the ship. After another thirty seconds, the metal bulkhead wall to their left stopped. There was a gap, allowing them to see across to the port deck. Lili, Lukas and Sami stood there. Lili had her weapon raised. Lukas was checking back the way they'd come. Sami was looking across at Max and Abby. Between the two groups was an external staircase leading to a separate enclosed area at the front of the ship. Max and Sami exchanged a glance and nodded. The two groups of cadets advanced towards each other and met at the bottom of the staircase.

'I think this is it,' Max said. 'There's nothing forward of this position, anyway. I vote we investigate.'

The others agreed.

'Cover me,' Max said. 'I'll get to the top of the staircase, see what's beyond that door up there.'

Lili knelt to one side of the staircase, pointing her weapon to the entrance at the top. Max climbed gingerly, holding tightly to a railing as the wind shook him from both sides. At the top he saw that the door had a round window, smeared with rain on the outside and condensation on the inside. He peered through it to see a well-lit corridor with another door at the end, five metres away. Looking over his shoulder, he made an 'I'm going in' gesture, then forced the heavy door open and stepped inside. As the door closed behind him, the sound of the wind was suddenly deadened. Dripping wet, and leaving a trail of water behind him, he advanced along the corridor. He reached the door at the far end and peered through a round window.

It was the bridge. That much was clear. He counted twelve men in total. Two were in military camouflage, the rest in black foul-weather gear. None of them had any weapons on display, but that didn't mean they weren't carrying. They all had their backs to Max. It was impossible to tell what they were saying or doing. But they hadn't seen Max, and that was the important thing.

He retreated quickly, back to the external door and down the staircase. The other cadets looked at him expectantly.

'That's it,' he said. 'I think it's the only way in.'

'How many people?' Lukas said.

'Twelve.'

'Armed?'

'Impossible to tell. But if we move quickly, I think we'll have the element of surprise. There are two guys in camouflage gear. I guess they're the ones most likely to be armed. Me and Lili will hold them at gunpoint. We'll tell the others to get to the ground. The rest of you, search the bridge for anything that gives us an idea of where the attack is going to be.'

'What if they're more heavily armed than we're expecting?' Sami said.

Max inhaled slowly before answering. 'Remember what that guy told us on the whale-watching boat?' he said. 'That three hundred and twenty-three Argentines died when the *Belgrano* was sunk? Remember the war memorial outside Government House, commemorating two hundred and fifty-five British dead? Remember what Hector told us, that what we're doing here could make the difference between war and peace?' He looked across the deck and over the dark, stormy ocean.

'Look out, you lot,' Abby muttered. 'He's going to say something heroic.'

'It just seems to me,' Max continued, 'that the lives of five teenagers would be a small price to pay to avoid history repeating itself.'

Sami jutted out his chin. 'It won't come to that,' he said. 'Because we're going to watch each other's backs, right?'

'Right,' the others said in unison, and they prepared to advance to target.

18

The Bridge

Max led the way.

His weapon was a part of him. An extension of his arm. If his body turned, so did his gun, always pointing in the direction he faced. He held it at shoulder height, two-handed. His finger rested just outside the trigger guard.

He pushed the first door open with his foot. The corridor was still empty. As he advanced to the bridge, he could sense Lili at his shoulder, her weapon raised in the same position. The other cadets followed.

At the entrance to the bridge they stopped. They moved their fingers from the trigger guard to the trigger. Max already knew that the door opened inwards. Either he or Lili needed to be the first to enter. They nodded an unspoken acknowledgement: it would be Max. Still gripping his weapon, he kicked the door open and entered.

The bridge had low windows extending around the front and both sides. Up ahead there was a bank of electronic navigation equipment: several screens of charts and weather information. There were two big leather chairs in front of the screens, and various complicated-looking boards of control instruments and radio gear. The lighting was low, but it was still difficult to see anything outside as the rain lashed against the windows.

Most of the men were at the front of the bridge, quietly staring out at the darkness outside. The two men in camouflage gear stood in the centre of the bridge, their backs to the door. It was clear that they expected no intrusion.

Nobody on the bridge even noticed Max was there until Lili was inside and standing next to him. They raised their weapons and each released a single round, carefully aimed at the ceiling. The double retort of the rounds punched across the bridge.

The two men in camouflage gear were the first to react. They spun around, digging their hands into their jackets to remove their weapons. But Max and Lili were already bearing down on them. Lili, whose linguistic skills were much better than Max's, shouted something in Spanish. The two soldiers dropped their weapons and, at another instruction from Lili, kicked them away.

The other cadets were on the bridge. Lukas and Abby snatched the two spare weapons. They cocked them expertly and ostentatiously, making it clear that they knew how to handle them. They took up position in the centre of the bridge, panning their stolen weapons around, as Lili shouted something else. The adults in the room looked at each other uncertainly. Lili shouted again and they all – including the guys in camouflage – lay on the ground and put their hands on the back of their heads.

'I think you get a 9 in Spanish,' Abby commented.

'Thanks,' Lili said. 'I've been practising.'

'Sami,' Max cut in, 'check the navigation screens, see what you can work out.'

There was a strange period of silence as Sami worked. It was broken only by a background hum, and the strange, deadened sound of the storm outside. Max, Lili, Lukas and Abby kept their weapons trained on the prostrate men. Sami wove his way through them to the navigation panels. He walked along the line of screens, examining each one in turn. 'Nothing,' he called over his shoulder. 'It's just current GPS location, weather charts . . .'

He was interrupted by a burst of sound from the VHF radio to the left-hand side of the navigation panel. A voice spoke over the airways in Spanish. They listened.

'What did he say?' Max asked when the voice fell silent.

'They're just requesting a radio check,' Lili replied.

'Do we reply?' Lukas asked.

'No,' Max said. 'Not yet. We need to find out the details of the attack and broadcast it on the emergency channel as soon as we can.'

'Look,' Sami said. There was an edge to his voice. He held up a paper chart, well-worn and folded in several places. It was a sepia colour, and it showed coastlines, depth soundings and tidal diamonds. A pale compass rose showed true north and magnetic north, and there were handwritten markings made in fine red and blue pen.

'What is it?' Lukas said.

'It's a nautical chart of the Falklands,' Sami replied. 'Look: Port Stanley, RAF Mount Pleasant . . .' He jabbed at areas on the map. 'These blue arrows here are pointing towards the cove where we saw the frogmen arriving. But these red arrows . . .' He pointed at an area further around the coastline, heading anticlockwise. 'They're pointing to a completely different landing area. Check out the depth soundings and tidal diamonds. It's a shallow beach with calm waters.'

'Perfect for an invasion force,' Max said.

'Right.'

'We need to transmit this information to HMS *Stirling*,' Max said. 'Sami, get on the VHF radio. Use emergency channel 16, it's –'

It happened before he could finish. As Max spoke to Sami, he and Lili had momentarily taken their attention from the two men in camouflage gear at their feet. But the men were alert. They rolled towards Max and Lili, grabbed them by the ankles and wrestled them to the floor. Max was taken by surprise. The gunman knelt on his chest. He held one hand over Max's throat while he slammed Max's gun hand hard on the floor several times. Max lost his grip on the gun, which slid across the floor. His assailant seized it.

There was a sudden hubbub in the room. Men were shouting in Spanish. Lukas and Abby screamed at them to stay down. But as Max's guy grabbed him by his throat and dragged him to his feet, Max sensed that the dynamic in the room had changed. The crew members were standing up. They seemed to be suddenly aware that, for all their screaming, Lukas and Abby were not going to shoot them. Sami was at the front of the bridge, clutching the nautical chart, desperately looking around, as though he might find something that would help them gain the upper hand again. But there was nothing. Lukas and Abby still had their weapons raised, but they were edging back to the exit.

Even as he felt the barrel of his handgun being pressed into the side of his head, Max shouted: '*Sami! Take the chart! Get back to the RIB! We'll hold them off!*'

Sami blinked. Max knew how reluctant Sami would be to leave the others in danger, that he would need urging.

'*Do it!*' he bellowed. '*Go! Now!*'

And as if to punctuate his instruction, Lukas and Abby each released a round from their weapons: not at the crew members on the bridge, but at the floor just in front of them. The rounds sparking off the metal floor was enough to make them disperse, and Sami took his chance. Chart in hand, he sprinted across the bridge towards the exit. One of the guys in camo gear yelled an instruction to follow him, but Sami was fast and he was skilful. In seconds, he was through the door and out of there.

The two guys in camouflage started shouting again, their guns still pressed to Max and Lili's heads.

'Follow him!' Max shouted. 'We have to make sure he gets away to warn someone . . .'

But he didn't need to say it. Lukas and Abby were still backing up towards the door, arms outstretched, panning their guns left and right to stop anyone getting too close.

Abby was looking at Max, her expression wretched at the prospect of leaving him and Lili in danger. Lukas, however, was looking elsewhere. One of the crew members had hurled himself towards the VHF radio. With a pang, Max realised that if he radioed for help, Sami's chance of warning the British that they were being fooled by a decoy force would be diminished.

But Lukas was already on it.

The crew member picked up the handset and was about to speak when Lukas released a third round in his direction. The round hit the radio handset, which burst into pieces in the man's hand. Lukas reoriented his weapon and fired another shot at the main body of the radio. There was a spark and a plume of smoke as the round hit. The VHF radio was disabled.

Lukas's precise shot had an immediate effect on the other crew members' confidence. They edged away, casting anxious sidelong glances at each other. It gave Lukas and Abby the opportunity to back further to the exit.

'*Go!*' Max hissed.

Lukas nodded curtly and left the bridge. Abby hesitated, her worried eyes lingering on Max. He mouthed the words 'We'll follow!' The guy holding him issued a harsh counter-instruction in Spanish, and jammed the handgun a little harder into the side of his head. Max ignored that. With obvious reluctance, Abby exited the bridge.

Which left Max, Lili and twelve enemy personnel.

Max and Lili faced each other on either side of the door, approximately four metres apart. Their assailants had them in a chokehold from behind, guns pressed to their heads. They were yelling instructions at the others – which meant they were not fully focused on restraining Max and Lili.

And that was their big mistake.

Because the Special Forces Cadets had trained for exactly this moment, and trained well.

Max and Lili knew that to counteract a rear chokehold they had to move fast, hard and at the same time. While their assailants were still shouting, the two cadets locked gazes, nodded, then struck.

They were a mirror image of each other as they performed three separate movements at the same time.

Movement one. Max yanked his right arm upwards, knocking the weapon that was pressed to his head out of position. The weapon fired. Max didn't know if the shot was deliberate or accidental, but it didn't matter; the round discharged harmlessly into the ceiling.

Movement two. With his left hand he grabbed the fingers of the arm that held him in a neck lock. Without hesitation, he yanked the man's fingers backwards. There was a cracking sound as the knuckle joints broke.

Movement three. Max stamped on his assailant's foot. The man shrieked in pain, but somehow still managed to keep his arm hooked around Max's neck. But that was okay, because Max had one more move. He jabbed his right elbow back as far as he could, knocking it hard into the man's solar plexus.

Meanwhile, Lili was doing exactly the same.

The men staggered backwards in shock. They still held

their weapons, but they were doubled over in pain, which gave the cadets a brief window to escape.

They seized it.

Ignoring the shouts from the other crew members, they hurtled to the exit and, once through, sprinted along the corridor. At the far end, Max pulled open the heavy external door, to be greeted by a sudden blast of wind and rain. But he'd battle the elements any day over the gunmen that he knew were following them. He let Lili run through, then exited the corridor himself, aware in his peripheral vision that crew members had already appeared at the other end. The door slammed behind him. Before he ran down the slippery external staircase, he saw the misted glass panel of the door crack and splinter as a round hit it from the inside.

'Run!' he shouted at Lili, who was already halfway down the stairs. 'They're coming. RUN!'

19

Under Tension

Max and Lili sprinted along the port deck. The wind howled. Every few paces, Max checked behind him. They were midship when they saw men following. They heard shouting. Max could tell that they were not only being followed from behind; the men had spread out and were also approaching the stern from the starboard deck.

Lukas appeared just ahead of them: legs apart for balance, weapon raised straight ahead of him, expression fierce.

'Split!' he roared.

Max and Lili parted, Max moving to the bulkhead, Lili to the railings. Their manoeuvre gave Lukas a direct shot towards the bow. He lowered the gun slightly and fired. There was a muzzle flash from the handgun's barrel and Max heard the tinny ricochet as the round pinged off the floor just behind him. More shouting. Looking over his shoulder again, he saw that their pursuers had stopped, held back by Lukas's warning shots.

'Go!' Lukas shouted at them.

They didn't hesitate, but sprinted past him as he released another round to hold the enemy back.

Seconds later they were at the stern. Sami was there, standing at the rail, tugging at the taut rope leading from the back of the trawler.

'It's our RIB,' Lili explained breathlessly. It was instantly clear that the rope was under too much tension, the drag too severe, for the cadets to be able to haul the RIB in. Sami looked panicked as Lukas and Abby appeared on either side of the stern, aiming their weapons back towards the two side decks. Lukas fired another round, but when Abby tried to do the same, her handgun clicked.

'*I'm out of ammo!*' she shouted. '*They're coming!*'

There was barely time to think. 'Grab the rope!' Max shouted. 'Slide down!'

The other cadets stared at him, their brows furrowed.

'Do it! Now! We can't hold them back! Whatever you do, don't let go of the rope!'

Lukas tried to fire his weapon again. A click. He too was out of ammo. That seemed to kick-start the cadets into action. Sami climbed over the stern railing, grasped the rope with two hands and swung one leg over it so that he was lying on top of the rope, facing the trawler. He immediately slid out of sight and down the rope. Lili climbed over the rail. She threw herself overboard in the same way.

'Get over!' Max shouted to Abby. 'Don't let go! I'm going to have to undo the knot . . .'

'No need,' Abby said, her eyes flashing. She produced a

knife in a black scabbard from somewhere about her person and handed it to Max. As he grabbed it, she took hold of the rope, swung her legs over the stern rail and disappeared into the darkness.

Which left only Max and Lukas. Max's friend was sprinting up to him, several men in pursuit. Lukas turned and chucked his empty handgun in their direction. It struck the lead guy hard in the face, halting him and his companions for a split second. But there were more crew fast approaching from the other side.

Distance of the nearest crew member: ten metres.

'GO!' Max roared. '*AND DON'T LET GO OF THE ROPE!*'

Lukas required no further urging. Like the three cadets before him, he hurled himself over the railing, seized the rope with both hands and slid away into the darkness . . .

Max was left alone. He didn't bother trying to count how many enemies were advancing towards him. He knew there were too many for him to escape, if they got their hands on him. He gripped the handle of the knife between his teeth, turned and clutched the rope with his left hand. The water below was stormy and threatening. He tried not to focus on it as he swung his legs over the stern rail. For a moment he remembered the kid on the whale-watching boat who had almost fallen in, but he was brought back to the moment when he felt his heel clip the hand of one of the crew members as his legs swung over. The taut rope bounced slightly as he fell onto it, gripping it with his free hand. He prepared to let himself slide down but he saw someone leaning over the stern rail. It was the guy with the red eyes, freed from the cargo container. Somehow he had managed to get hold of another weapon – a rifle – and he was aiming it at Max.

Max knew he only had a fraction of a second. He grabbed the knife handle, pulled the scabbard off with his teeth and, clutching the rope as tightly as he could with his free hand, slashed the rope just above him.

The blade was wickedly sharp. It cut the rope as if it was butter. Max let the knife fall into the ocean and seized the leading end of the rope with his free hand. He didn't hear the sound of gunfire from the rifle, but he saw the muzzle flash as the guy with the red eyes took a shot at him.

He missed.

Because Max was falling.

The forward momentum of the trawler immediately distanced it from Max. His stomach lurched as he fell towards the ocean, clutching the rope, bracing himself for impact with the water . . .

He told himself to prepare for the cold water shock. He knew it would make his body instinctively want to suck in air, so he clamped his mouth shut.

It only took him a couple of seconds to fall. His body slapped painfully against the water, and then he was under.

The water was icy. Even though he was expecting it, the shock was profound, the urge to inhale almost overwhelming. Max felt as though every muscle in his body was clenched in his attempt to keep his mouth shut and his grip on the rope tight. But he was sinking fast. Sami, Abby and Lili had life jackets. He and Lukas had none. The roar of the storm and the trawler's engines were suddenly deadened by the water, and he found himself confused and disorientated. Which way was up? He didn't know. He would have liked to blow bubbles and see which way they rose, but it was impossibly dark. Instead, still clutching the rope, he raised his hands to his mouth and blew. He felt the bubbles rising and started to kick for the surface.

His lungs burned through lack of oxygen. The shock was turning to panic. Surely he should have reached the surface by now. What if he was swimming the wrong way? The currents were strong and confusing. Had they deceived him? Was he going to drown?

He felt his grip on the rope loosening. He had to force himself to hold on tighter as he continued to kick.

And suddenly, without warning, he broke the surface.

It was no longer silent. The sound of the wind and rain crashed all around him. The swell was immense. He inhaled deeply in relief. He couldn't see the trawler, the other cadets or their RIB – just mountains of water, shape-shifting all around him. Salt water gushed into his mouth as he breathed. He choked it out. As the swell lowered, he caught sight of the trawler, which was already a good distance away. Desperately treading water to keep above the surface, he wrapped the rope several times around his forearm to avoid losing hold of it. Because if that happened, he was dead: no question.

He started to haul himself along the rope. It was perhaps the hardest thing he'd ever done. His heavy, saturated clothes threatened to drag him down. He was expending as much energy simply keeping afloat as he was following the line of the rope. He could feel his muscles seizing up from the cold. But he knew he couldn't stop. Every now and then the rope came under tension, pulling him in an unexpected direction. He thought about his friends. Were they okay? Were they still holding the rope? Had they reached the RIB? Were they in trouble?

That thought gave him a surge of energy. He powered breathlessly through the water, occasionally going under but always breaking the surface again as he pulled himself along the rope. He had no idea how much time had passed. All he could do was keep moving, waterlogged, blinded and half drowned . . .

And then he saw it: the RIB, perhaps twenty metres away, suddenly appearing above the ocean swell. There were figures on board. He only saw them for a second before the RIB disappeared again. But the sight had lit a fire in Max's chest. He had more strength. More focus. He pulled himself along the rope with every ounce of vigour he had, until, a minute later, the RIB reappeared, almost close enough to touch, and he could hear his friends shouting at him . . .

Sudden silence. He'd been dragged under. He kicked himself up again, breaking the surface with another great inhalation of air. He felt hands grabbing his wet coat. Looking up, he saw Lukas and Sami's faces, fierce and determined. They were leaning over the edge of the RIB, hauling him up.

And then he was in the vessel, lying on his back, gasping for air, the others looking down at him as the boat rocked in the waves. He sat up groggily, his body shaking badly.

Before he knew what was happening, Abby had thrown herself at him and was kissing him frantically – his lips, his forehead, even his eyelids.

'If we could just drag you two apart?' Lili shouted above the elements, her eyes fiery.

'Right!' Abby shouted. 'Mind on the job. We need to make that distress call . . .'

'We can't!' Lukas bellowed. He was at the RIB's small radio station. 'The battery's down. I can't get the radio to work.' He slammed the unit with his fist in frustration.

Max staggered to his feet. 'We need to do something to stop the real attack,' he yelled.

'Maybe we can find HMS *Stirling*,' Abby suggested.

Max shook his head. 'We've no idea where it is. Even if we did, we can't risk approaching it in case they mistake us for an enemy vessel . . .'

A wave caught the side of the RIB and a cloud of spray covered them. Max gripped the side of the boat as it listed heavily. Once it was on an even keel, he heard Lili shouting.

'We only have one option! We have to head to the location of the real invasion. Maybe once we're there we can do something to stop it!'

The cadets stared at her. What she'd said sounded crazy. If there was a full invasion force heading unopposed towards the Falklands, what could *they* do about it?

On the other hand, what *else* could they do? Nothing? Could they just let the invasion happen?

'Sami!' Max shouted. 'Do you still have the chart?'

Sami nodded. He undid his wetsuit and pulled out the

chart he'd stolen from the bridge of the trawler. It was damp. The arrows marked in red and blue pen were smudged. But it was legible, just.

'We don't have any GPS,' Lukas shouted.

'Compass?' Max said.

Lukas nodded and pointed to the compass fixed in front of the steering wheel.

'Do we know our approximate position?'

'We know roughly where the trawler was when we left the *Stirling*,' Lili said. 'We can do a dead reckoning. It won't be completely accurate, but we can use it to work out a rough bearing.'

Max and his friends were dripping wet, bedraggled, shivering and exhausted. But right now, they were the only people who had any chance of preventing a major military invasion.

Quite how they were going to manage that, Max didn't know.

But they had to try.

'Let's do it,' he said.

20

Flare

Lili had the helm. Concentration was etched on her face as the RIB sliced through the dark waves. The other cadets gripped the sides, especially Max and Lukas, who had no life jackets to keep them afloat if they went over. The RIB felt tiny amid the immense swell of the ocean. Spray stung their faces and blinded them. The motor was barely audible above the vicious howling of the wind.

They had calculated that they needed to travel in a south-westerly direction. It was a gamble. Their calculations could be wrong. It would hardly be a surprise if their estimated position was way off. There were no landmarks here in the open sea from which to take bearings. They were motoring blind and there was every chance that they were heading not back to the Falklands but out to open sea.

Max banished those thoughts. They'd made their call and Lili was doing what she could to keep a steady course in fierce seas. He kept a keen lookout. If they had a man overboard, it would be sudden and silent. Vigilance was crucial. And he kept glancing ahead, desperately scanning the night sky in the hope of spotting land.

So far – nothing.

He was shivering. The cold bit his skin. His extremities were numb. He had to force himself to stay sharp. It was a great effort. Time was dragging and a dull sensation of panic was rising in his gut . . .

'Land!'

It was Sami who shouted. Max wiped salt from his eyes. He could just see a dark outline of land against the horizon. It disappeared as the sea swelled. When it reappeared seconds later, it was clearer, more obvious. The sight seemed to warm Max from his core. He thought he could see relief in the others' faces. They had only been at sea for a few hours, but it felt like a lifetime.

Lili kept her course. The land grew nearer. Max tried to estimate its distance, but it was difficult over stormy water and at night. A couple of miles, maybe?

'Are there binoculars?' he shouted.

Abby pointed to the storage unit. He found them and put them to his eyes, gripping the side of the RIB with his free hand. The rocking of the boat made it difficult to focus on the land. It jumped in and out of sight, a rocky headland appearing then disappearing.

And then . . .

'Stop!' Max shouted. 'Stop the boat! I've just seen something!'

Lili pulled back on the throttle. The boat slowed and she

turned it into the wind. Max stood up and looked through the binoculars again, checking that he hadn't been mistaken.

It was there, quite clear despite the darkness. Between the RIB and the headland, no more than five hundred metres away, he guessed, was the unmistakable outline of a submarine's conning tower. He spun around, panning along the horizon with the binoculars. He saw two other conning towers: one off to starboard, the other to stern.

'Subs!' he shouted. 'Big ones! I think we're in the middle of the attack force!'

As he spoke, one of the conning towers started to submerge.

'Do you think they saw us?' Lili yelled.

'I don't know. We need to get to land as fast as we can.'

Lili nodded. 'Hold on!'

Max crouched as she increased the throttle and the RIB surged forward. He kept scanning the surrounding area through the binoculars. There was suddenly no sign of the conning towers. He felt a flash of panic at the thought that there could be a submarine directly beneath them, ready to surface. If that happened, and it hit the RIB, it would be game over.

Distance to land: three hundred metres. Max checked the shoreline. There was a wide shingle beach. It sloped down at a shallow gradient, which he knew would continue into the water. Not that it mattered. Max knew from bitter experience how close a fleet of minisubs could get to the shore.

'Lights!' Sami shouted. He pointed to stern and slightly to starboard. Sure enough, there were lights on the horizon:

another ship, or maybe the one they'd just escaped. It didn't matter either way. As he raised his binoculars again, he saw – fleetingly – a flotilla of RIBs. They were loads of them – perhaps forty, or even more – and they were speeding towards the shore that was the cadets' destination.

'RIBs incoming!' he screamed. 'Lili, does this thing go any faster?'

But the throttle lever was fully forward. They could do nothing but keep travelling in a straight line to the shore and hope that the attack RIBs were no faster than theirs.

A hundred metres to the shore.

Fifty.

Max's skin prickled. He looked back towards the attack force of RIBs. They were definitely approaching the same location. As the cadets came within ten metres of the shore, Lukas raised the outboard motor. The vessel's momentum pushed it towards the shingle. As they beached, Lili spun the steering wheel so they turned 90 degrees to starboard. There was the grinding sound of the boat on shingle. Max had a profound urge to hurl himself off the boat – he'd seen enough of the ocean for a lifetime. First, however, he opened up the storage cabinet and withdrew the three emergency flares. Then, with his friends, he jumped onto the beach and sprinted inland.

Their feet sank in the shingle, slowing them down. Max could see the RIBs approaching shore. They were no more than a hundred metres out – but he could see something else too. Even closer to the beach, he saw the outline of minisubs, too numerous to count. He went cold all over as he remembered his horrific experience earlier that night. He forced himself to focus on their current situation. If each RIB and each minisub held six men, there had to be several hundred enemy soldiers about to attack the island, and the British had no idea of what was happening.

The beach became scrubland – easier to run on. They sprinted another hundred metres up to the brow of the hill, then threw themselves to the ground on its far side, breathing heavily, hiding themselves from view.

'What do we do now?' Abby gasped.

'We've got to warn someone,' Lili said. 'Anyone.'

'How, though?' Lukas asked. 'We've got no comms, and the British think the attack is happening over there.' He pointed to the south-east, in the direction of the cove they had first been assigned to watch.

'We could sprint there and tell them,' Sami said. 'I reckon it'll take us, what, half an hour . . .'

'That'll be too late,' Lukas said. 'The attack force will have made land already, and who knows what kind of weaponry they've cached here?'

'We can't just watch it happen,' Abby said. 'They're not here for a picnic. People are going to die.'

'Not if I've got anything to do with it,' Max said quietly.

The other cadets stared at him.

'He's got that look in his eye,' Abby said. 'You know, the one when he's about to do something clever.'

'Not really,' Max said. 'It's just the only option we have.' He held up the flares he'd taken from the RIB. 'We need to set these off,' he said. 'Right now. They'll be seen for miles around. It'll bring the attention of the British to this exact location. They'll work out what it means.'

'Er, Max,' Abby said, frowning. 'You realise that if we do that, we'll give away our precise position to hundreds of soldiers who'd quite like – and I'm just guessing here – to kill us immediately?'

'Yeah,' Max said. 'Actually, I do.'

'Got any clever suggestions what we do about that?'

'Just one.'

'Uh-huh?'

'Run,' Max said. 'Like, really fast. As soon as they're on land, they're an infantry force. They're no faster than us. If we can outrun them, we stay safe.'

'Not that safe,' Lukas said. 'They'll be armed.'

'And I feel like I've done enough running for a lifetime,' Lili said.

Max inclined his head to concede the points. 'Any better ideas? Now's the time to speak up.'

Nobody spoke. Max took their silence as approval.

There were three flares. Max knew that they would be seen from land, from sea and from the sky, if it came to that. Each one would send a red flare about three hundred metres into the sky, where it would burn for approximately forty seconds. If they launched all three at the same time, it would be quite a display. He handed one to Lili and one to Lukas. Then he peered over the hill.

His mouth went dry as he saw what was approaching.

It looked as if a full army was emerging from the sea. Hundreds of men, seawater cascading from their helmets and their camouflage gear, weapons slung across their chests. The ocean was dotted with RIBs, and the military force was already advancing up the beach towards the cadets.

Max threw himself back to the ground. He lay on his back and pointed his flare towards the sky. 'They're coming,' he hissed. 'Hundreds of them. We have to fire the flares!'

Lili and Lukas adopted the same position. They each held the body of their flare with one hand, the other hand untwisting the cap at the bottom and clutching the firing tab.

'NOW!' Max shouted. They pulled the tabs, releasing the flares in unison. There was a sudden *whoosh* as the charges forced the handheld fireworks high into the sky. A moment of silence. And then – *bang*. The three flares illuminated in quick succession, so bright that they hurt Max's eyes. Even though the flares were in the air, they bathed the cadets in a dusky red light. Max was glad they were on the ground, because otherwise they would be lit up on the hill: easy targets for the soldiers barely a hundred metres away.

'We have to run!' Lili hissed. The other cadets nodded fervently.

'Which direction?' Lukas demanded.

'I'm thinking, as far away as possible,' Abby said. 'Let's just get out of here.'

She started to scramble away from the shoreline, keeping low to avoid being seen by the incoming force. The others followed. Except Max. They'd only gone a few metres when Abby looked back over her shoulder and saw that he hadn't moved.

'Come on!' she urged.

He shook his head. 'I have to do something else.'

The cadets stared at him. 'What?' Sami said.

'It's not just an infantry attack,' Max said. 'It's an airborne attack too. We know that because of the transponder at the listening station. It's got to be destroyed, otherwise the island's vulnerable to an air strike.'

Sami shook his head. 'You can't,' he said, eyes wide. 'The attack is under way. They could launch a strike on the listening station at any moment. If you're in the vicinity . . .'

Max gave him a half-smile. 'Yeah,' he said. 'Wouldn't want to do anything dangerous, huh?'

Sami wasn't amused. 'You'll be killed, Max. You have to stay with us.'

Max narrowed his eyes. 'Not going to happen, Sami.' He glanced in the direction of the oncoming force. 'You guys don't get away scot-free though. You need to make sure nobody's following me. You get what I'm saying?'

'You want us to act as a decoy?' Lili said.

'Right. Can you do it?'

Grim-faced, Lili, Sami and Lukas nodded. Abby, though, shook her head. 'I'm coming with you,' she said.

'No.'

'Don't argue, Max. We set off three flares. It'll make sense to the invaders if they see three of us. More than that, they'll start wondering if there are others.'

Max started to disagree, but Abby wasn't having it. 'We have to go,' she urged, pointing back towards the shore. 'They'll be on us any second.'

'She's right,' said Lukas, frowning. 'If we're going to do

this, we have to do it now.' He turned to Max and Abby. 'Go,' he said.

Max hesitated, but before he knew what was happening, Abby had grabbed his wrist. They hurtled off together over the scrubland, keeping low as they ran up a shallow incline in what Max thought was an easterly direction. He reckoned they were two miles from the listening station. He could only pray that they got there in time.

They'd been running for a minute when they stopped to look back. They could just see the beach, covered with the sinister shadow of the invading force. And they could see the other cadets – Lukas, Lili and Sami – still crouching. They had been waiting there to give their friends the chance to get away. But now, as Max and Abby watched, the others suddenly stood up and started sprinting to the south.

When their heads became visible above the brow of the hill, the shooting started.

21

Zigzag

Lukas knew they'd left it too late.

They'd given Max and Abby a full minute to get away, and now they were paying the price. The first bullet passed over his head the moment they stood up and started running away from the beach. He didn't dare stop to check how close the soldiers were. Anything that slowed them down, even for a second, could be fatal.

More gunfire. Lukas felt a round whizz over his right shoulder. He sensed Sami and Lili separating from him. They had been running too close together. Spread out, they would divide the attack force's firepower into three. And now, with his two friends at least fifteen metres away on either side, he heard Hector's harsh voice in his head. *If you're running from an armed shooter, move in a zigzag. That way, you present a target moving laterally, which is harder to hit. And for God's sake tuck your head down, so you turn yourself into a smaller target.*

Lukas instantly altered his trajectory slightly to the left. At that moment, a round almost brushed his right arm. Not for the first time, Lukas silently thanked the training they'd been given back in Valley House. He zigzagged to the left, upping his pace. The wind was behind them, and he felt it gave him a little more speed. When another round passed over his head, he sensed that the shooter was further away than before.

He heard Lili's voice. 'Over there!'

Lukas glanced in the direction she was pointing. The land sloped downhill. It would take them out of the shooters' line of fire, at least momentarily. The three cadets headed towards the dip, still keeping their distance from each other and zigzagging. The gunfire had stopped. Lukas assumed they were out of sight. He didn't know how long that would last.

It was still raining and the ground had become marshy underfoot. Lili was leading them along a thin stream that wound its way from up in the hills beyond. The cadets were soaked, so the mud seeping through their shoes barely made a difference. There were hillocks on either side. Lukas considered using them as cover. He was mindful of their strategy: they were a decoy, leading members of the attack force away from Max and Abby. They needed to stay out of range of the shooters, but still draw them in this direction . . .

With that in mind, Lukas looked back. That was his mistake.

He could just discern the outline of a man, perhaps a hundred metres away. Then his foot hit something hard. He fell, twisting his ankle as he did so, and shouted in pain.

He tried to scramble back to his feet, but as soon as he attempted to put any weight on his right foot, a shock of agony screamed up his leg. He collapsed to the ground again.

Lili and Sami reached him within seconds. They urged him to his feet and he gave it another go. It was no good. He couldn't stand unaided. Wincing with pain, he looked back towards the advancing figure.

'Leave me,' he hissed. 'You need to get out of here. They'll be on us any moment.'

Something passed between Lili and Sami. They nodded, then gently manoeuvred Lukas back to the ground. Without another word, they disappeared.

Lukas gasped for breath. The pain in his foot was intense and his lungs burned. A tiny part of him questioned whether he should be surprised that his two friends had left him here. He banished that thought from his mind. They'd done what they needed to do. There was no point all three of them dying. Lukas's survival was up to him now. Screwing up his face, he tried to crawl. Perhaps if he could find a hiding place – a depression in the ground, or a bush, anything . . .

But, apart from the hillocks on either side, there was nothing. No cover. No escape.

He felt that perhaps the pain was easing a little, and he made another attempt to get to his feet. He was a little steadier now. He couldn't run, but he might be able to hobble. If he could get over the nearest hillock, perhaps he had a chance . . .

He looked back again. The figure was there. Twenty metres away, no more. He had his weapon raised, the butt of his rifle pressed into his shoulder. Lukas blinked in astonishment. He recognised the soldier with red eyes. They sent a shock of fear through his gut. How had he got here? He must have launched a RIB from the trawler. His lip was curled into a sneer and there was no doubt in Lukas's mind that that his enemy recognised him.

Nor was there any doubt about what he intended to do.

Lukas staggered back, his arms raised in surrender. The soldier approached. Ten metres. Five. His weapon was aimed at Lukas's chest. He was moving his finger from the trigger guard to the trigger. Getting ready to squeeze it.

He spat something in Spanish, then stared at Lukas, as if relishing what he was about to do.

Unfortunately for the soldier, he was too focused on what stood in front of him to pay attention to what was approaching from behind.

Sami and Lili had emerged from the cover of the hillock. They moved silently, and so fast that the soldier didn't know what had hit him. Lili went low, diving at the soldier's ankles and pulling his feet out from underneath him. As soon as he tumbled, Sami dived on his body, smothering it and pointing the weapon in a safe direction. The soldier discharged a round, deafeningly loud because it was so close, but it shot harmlessly off into the night.

Lukas could do nothing but watch as his two friends ruthlessly dealt with the soldier. Sami unclipped the weapon from his chest and handed it to Lili. While she made it safe, Sami raised one fist and inclined his head slightly. 'I'm extremely sorry about this,' he said, his voice quite earnest, before slamming his fist hard onto the soldier's neck: once, twice, a third time before the soldier's eyes glazed over and he went limp. Sami and Lili turned to Lukas.

'You okay?' Sami asked. He was out of breath.

Lukas nodded, then winced as he tried to walk.

Sami stood up and pointed at the soldier at his feet. 'I don't know how long he'll be out,' he said. 'Maybe no more than a few minutes. And his mates might be searching for him.'

'Can you walk?' Lili asked Lukas.

'I'll do my best,' Lukas said. He pointed ahead of him. 'We'll keep going that way, yes?'

'As fast as we can.' Lili pointed back the way they'd come. 'Look.' There were more figures on the horizon, heading in their direction.

Lukas set his jaw. He held on to Sami for support and started to limp as quickly as he could. 'Come on,' he said. 'What are you waiting for?'

Max's heart beat fast. His lungs burned. He was running on adrenaline and nervous energy. He and Abby ran side by side, soaked to the skin, gusts of wind trying to knock them to the ground.

'How much further?' Abby shouted.

Max didn't know. A mile? Maybe a little more? 'Just keep running!' he yelled. 'We have to get to that transponder!'

As he spoke, he saw something in the distance that chilled him. Lights in the sky. An aircraft. Could it be a fast air attack? Were they too late?

'It's a helicopter!' Abby shouted. 'It's coming from the RAF base. Look, there's more than one. They must be reacting to the flares.'

Max wiped rain from his eyes as he ran and squinted in the direction of the lights. There were several helicopters speeding towards them. Even if Abby was right, however, and they had been alerted by the flares, Max couldn't allow himself a feeling of relief. His instinct told him that an Argentine air strike was still imminent. They *had* to get to the transponder.

They upped their pace. Suddenly, the choppers were very close. There were five. Each had a searchlight scouring the landscape. The powerful lights illuminated the driving rain that swirled and eddied across the sky. As the choppers flew overhead, Max and Abby threw themselves to the ground. They didn't want to be spotted. It would be too easy for the helicopter crews to mistake them for invaders. They pressed themselves into the rough grass as the searchlights fell on them, the rotors of the chopper deafeningly loud, the downdraught stronger even than the wind. But they were gone in a second, hurtling towards the site of the invasion . . .

The two cadets pushed themselves to their feet and continued to run, battling through the elements and ignoring their own exhaustion. Max could see a fence up ahead. It looked like the boundary of a minefield and he thought he recognised where they were.

'We're close!' he shouted to Abby. 'Keep going!'

They ran hard.

'Choppers!' Sami shouted.

They were approaching fast.

'They're coming from the RAF base, I think,' Lili yelled. 'They must have seen the flares. Get down! We don't want them to mistake us for invaders!'

They hit the ground. Lukas winced with pain. As the helicopters passed over, their searchlights lit up the ground all around them. After they had passed, Lukas rolled over and looked back. He was searching for the soldier Sami had knocked unconscious. There was no sign of him. Lukas was relieved.

It was short-lived.

As soon as the helicopters had thundered past, the dark outline of a figure rose on the horizon. Lukas felt a sick feeling in the pit of his stomach. He knew it was the red-eyed soldier. He had regained consciousness, and was now staggering towards them.

Lili had his weapon. Lukas glanced at it meaningfully. 'Fire some warning shots!'

But Lili was already kneeling in the firing position, ready to lay down suppressing rounds. She cocked the weapon with a dull clunk and aimed it carefully. Lukas prepared himself for the sound of gunfire.

It didn't come. There was just an impotent click from the weapon.

'Stoppage,' Lili hissed.

'We don't have time to strip it down,' Sami said. 'Look, he's coming. We have to –'

The word 'move' was drowned out by a crack of gunfire coming from the soldier. *'He's got a handgun!'* Lukas shouted. 'We have to get away from him!'

Sami and Lili pulled Lukas to his feet. A sharp pain ran up his leg. Every step he took was agonising, even with his friends' help. Behind him, the soldier was advancing implacably. He fired another shot, and Lukas could tell that the round had fallen just short of them. The handgun was moving into range.

To their right, the land undulated.

'That way!' Lukas pointed. 'It'll give us cover.'

'How long for?' Sami said grimly.

'Maybe enough time to clear the stoppage on the rifle.'

'We can't shoot him,' Sami said.

'We might not have a choice.'

'I don't think we'll have enough time,' Lili said. 'He's moving pretty fast for a guy who was unconscious a few minutes ago.'

'I should have hit him harder,' Sami muttered. 'He'd be safer that way.'

'*We'd* be safer that way,' Lili said. 'He'll kill us if he gets close enough.'

They struggled to the top of the next hill. The pain in Lukas's leg was insane. As they hurried downhill, he stumbled and fell to his knees with a cry of agony.

Then he saw something.

Twenty metres away was a fence. It was identical to the fence that had cordoned off the birdwatching area they had visited with Peter. One of the upright wooden posts was set at a 45-degree angle to the ground, as though falling. Just to its right was a red metal sign. It said: 'Danger: Mines'.

Lukas narrowed his eyes. He glanced from the sign to the wooden post, and then to a patch of low brush twenty metres from their position.

'I've got an idea,' he said.

22

Incoming

'There it is!' Max shouted. 'The listening station!'

They were running alongside the birdwatching area where the albatross had visited them. Max felt a tingle of fear in the side of his body closest to the minefield. He put the minefield out of his mind and, Abby at his side, hurtled towards the concrete structure.

Morning was coming. There was no sign of the sun – it was too overcast. Just a faint lightening of the sky. It allowed the outline of the listening station to emerge more clearly, like a ghostly figure stepping out of the mist.

Abby suddenly grabbed Max by the wrist, forcing him to stop.

'What are you doing?' he demanded.

'I just wanted to say . . .' Abby whispered. Her wet hair was plastered to her face, her eyes very wide. 'We could be running straight into an airstrike, and if it hits before we can destroy the transponder . . .'

'We have to go, Abby.'

'I know. I just wanted to tell you . . .' She held out one hand and touched his cheek.

'I know,' Max said. He gave her a warm smile. 'Me too . . .' He looked towards the listening post. 'We need to . . .'

'On it,' Abby said. She grinned at him and pushed the wet hair off her face. They started to run again.

The hole that Max had found in the fence was still there. The two cadets passed through it and sprinted along the path that led down to the station. Max's whole body was tingling now. He had to repress the urge to turn and run in the opposite direction. He and Abby were putting themselves in danger, making themselves a target. But they didn't have an option. They kept running.

And they were only halfway to the listening station when they heard it.

It was very distant, but unmistakable: a boom that reverberated above the sound of the wind and the rain. Max and Abby stopped for a moment, breathless, staring at each other.

'Oh my God,' Abby said. 'Fast air.'

Max nodded. 'Fast air,' he agreed. 'Incoming.'

Lukas couldn't put his plan into action himself. He wasn't mobile enough. He had to observe, crouched on the wet earth, as Sami kept watch at the brow of the incline, and Lili got to work.

The wonky wooden post was clearly rotten. That was why it failed to stay upright. So when Lili ran up to it, it took only a few moments to yank it from its setting and force it to lie flat on the earth. As she did this, Lukas watched with satisfaction as the wire fencing on either side collapsed with the post. It served two purposes. Anyone stumbling across the scenario would think that someone had pulled down the fence in order to cross it. And the 'Danger: Mines' sign was now face-down on the ground, invisible to anybody who was not looking for it.

'He'll be here in less than a minute!' Sami hissed.

The trap was set. Lukas hobbled over to the area of low brush, helped along by Sami. Lili ran to it from the fence. Together, they lay on their fronts amid the wet, spiky foliage. It was deeply uncomfortable, but once again Lukas could hear Hector's voice in his mind. *The best place to hide is the most uncomfortable. Look for a location where nobody would want to venture.* As a thorn pressed into the side of his face, it occurred to Lukas that Hector would approve.

Then they saw him. The soldier appeared at the top of the incline. His red eyes seemed to burn in the dawn light. He clutched his handgun in both hands. He scanned the area, plainly looking for the cadets. For an awful moment, Lukas thought his gaze had settled on their hiding place. He held his breath, making certain he didn't move even a millimetre. The soldier scanned past their position and, after what felt like an age, his eyes fell on the collapsed fence. Squinting, Lukas could see the expression on his face: a dismissive sneer. He thought he could interpret the soldier's thoughts: that he now knew how to find the three stupid kids who had attacked him . . .

The soldier stepped forward. He was unsteady on his feet, as though he hadn't fully recovered from Sami's brutal punches. Still clutching his weapon, he staggered down the hill towards the fence. Lukas swallowed hard. Despite everything – the murder of the old farmer, the death threats he'd given Lukas and Max – he didn't want the soldier to step on an anti-personnel mine. Surely there wouldn't be any so close to the perimeter fence. Whoever erected it would have included a buffer zone. Still, he felt a metallic chill down his spine as the soldier climbed over the fallen fence, lifting his legs high to avoid the roll of barbed wire. And he held his breath as the man headed into the minefield.

He was ten metres beyond the perimeter fence when Lukas said: 'Now.'

There was no decision-making time. It was a reflex action. Max and Abby ran. Not away from the listening station, to where they had a chance – a small chance – of finding safety. But towards it, knowing that the boom they'd heard in the distance was a fast air strike, and they were at ground zero.

Within seconds, they were alongside the building. Max led the way to the transponder. The painted iron door was there, and the concrete block in front of it. He could see the dim red light of the transponder glowing. At the same time, he could hear the roar of the fast air approaching. He knew that in the time it took him to cover the handful of metres between him and the transponder, the aircraft would travel hundreds of metres. He threw himself towards the transponder with no clear idea of how he was going to disable the device.

Then he was alongside it. He gripped it in both hands and gritted his teeth as he desperately tried to pull it away from the concrete block.

It wouldn't budge.

The roar of the aircraft was getting louder. It was close, ready to take out the listening station. Rain and sweat trickled into Max's eyes as he desperately tried to yank the transponder away from its fixings . . .

But he couldn't.

'Move!' Abby shouted.

Max glanced to his left. She stood by his side, straining to lift a football-sized rock above her head.

'*MOVE!*' she repeated. '*NOW!*'

Lili stood up. She had the assault rifle. She pointed it at the soldier's back. It had a stoppage, of course, but he didn't know that.

'Hey!' she shouted. 'Over here!'

The soldier spun around as Lukas and Sami got to their feet. His eyes widened as the facts of his situation dawned on him. The three cadets were out of range of his handgun, whereas he was very much in the line of fire of Lili's assault rifle.

'Tell him he's in a minefield,' Lukas said. 'Tell him that if he takes even a single step, he could stand on an anti-personnel mine.'

Lili translated Lukas's words into Spanish. She had to shout, because in the distance there was the boom of an aircraft. Lukas and Sami exchanged a worried look. Lukas knew what that noise had to be: fast air, coming in to launch a strike on the listening station. He felt his mouth turn dry as he thought of Max and Abby, heading straight into the danger zone. If the aircraft was incoming, surely that meant they had failed to destroy the transponder in time . . .

Focus, Lukas told himself. *Trust them to do their job . . .*

He turned back to the soldier. Had he understood Lili's words? Had he even heard them above the roar of the aircraft? There was no way of knowing, but Lukas had a bad feeling. The man was eyeing the three cadets with a look of obvious incredulity. A look that said: kids, handling an assault rifle? They won't know how to fire it accurately. And even if they do, they'd never dare . . .

The soldier kept his handgun raised and took a step towards them.

Lili screamed at him again in Spanish. This time there was no doubt that her words went unheard because it sounded as if the fast air was right above them, even though they couldn't see anything through the clouds. It was so loud that they didn't even hear the retort of the soldier's handgun as he fired and walked. They only knew that he had discharged a round because they saw the recoil of his weapon.

They didn't even hear the sound of the mine exploding when he stepped on it.

They certainly saw its effects.

As long as he lived, Lukas would never forget the sight. The blast sent chunks of earth fountaining into the air. The shocking, grisly sight of their enemy's limbs, detached from his body, flying through the air and raining down on the damp ground would stay with the cadets for ever.

'GET DOWN!' Lili roared as the shrapnel fell. She pulled Lukas to the ground, where he instinctively covered the back of his head with his arms.

'What about Max and Abby?' he yelled, his voice muffled. 'The air strike! It's here! It's going to hit them!'

Nobody replied. There was nothing to say.

'*MOVE,*' Abby shouted. '*NOW!*'

Max blinked and stepped back.

Not a second too soon.

It was as if Abby was unable to hold the rock up any longer. She let the rock fall hard on the body of the transponder. It broke away from the concrete with a spark, and its red light extinguished. The device's casing fell to the ground, where it shattered.

Abby had gripped Max's wrist and was pulling him away. It wasn't necessary. Every fibre of Max's being wanted to get away from that listening station now that the transponder was destroyed. He ran with her, away from the concrete block, away from the listening station, his lungs and muscles burning as they sprinted as fast as possible, not knowing if they'd destroyed the device in time to stop the strike.

The noise of the aircraft overhead seemed to be inside him, rattling his organs.

Max and Abby stopped. They looked at each other. Then they looked up. The noise of the aircraft was receding. It had passed, and it had not dropped its payload. They had destroyed the transponder in time.

There was a strange, deep silence.

Relief crashed over them. They took a moment to catch their breath, then they looked at each other and embraced.

'Do you think we've stopped the invasion?' Abby said. Her voice was small. Uncertain. 'Do you think we've done enough?'

As if in response, there was a new sound in the sky. More helicopters, heading from the direction of the RAF base.

Max didn't let her go. He couldn't. Their embrace was warm and comforting, here in the dawn drizzle after such a night.

'Yeah,' he said. 'I think we've done enough.'

Epilogue

They *had* done enough. Or so it seemed to Max.

The sun continued to rise and the air filled with the buzzing of helicopters. Max and Abby, exhausted, collapsed on the grass at the perimeter fence and watched them fly over. It was clear that they had two destinations: some were heading to the decoy landing site, some to the real one. There would be no time for the invaders to locate their caches, dig out their anti-aircraft weapons and whatever other instruments of war they had been stashing on the island over time. Their invasion was surely over before it had even begun.

'Do you think we should check on the others?' Abby asked in a small voice. She sounded as drained as Max felt.

'We should stay here,' Max said. 'We don't want anybody mistaking us for the wrong people. We've done our bit.'

'I hope they're okay.'

'Yeah,' Max said. 'Me too.'

Abby leaned her head against Max's shoulder. After a second, Max put his arm around her. They stayed like that for a couple of silent minutes, drawing warmth and comfort from each other.

'I thought you and Lukas were dead,' Abby said finally. Her voice cracked. 'I really did.'

'If it wasn't for you guys,' Max replied, 'we would be. Thank you.'

'Ah, it's nothing. What's a quick life-saving between friends, anyway?' She shuffled up so they were face to face, their noses almost touching. Max felt her breath hot against his lips, which were parted slightly.

'Er, I hate to tell you this,' Max whispered, 'but I think we're being watched.'

He felt her tense up. They both turned.

A man was standing ten metres away. He had a ruddy, friendly face, sandy hair, a nose that had once been broken and a mischievous smile playing on his lips.

'Morning, chaps,' said Woody, his hair blowing in the breeze. 'Not interrupting, am I?'

Max felt himself blushing. Abby raised an eyebrow, but showed no sign of embarrassment. 'Perfect timing,' she said in a voice that barely hid her irritation with the Watcher.

Woody's face lit up. 'Excellent!' he said. 'The others will be here in a minute.'

'Are they okay?' Max said, standing. He held out a hand to help Abby up, but she brushed it away.

'What am I?' she muttered. 'Incompetent?'

'Hardly that,' Woody said. 'The others are fine. Angel's found them. Lukas has been in the wars, but they're all in one piece.' He walked towards them. 'Seriously, guys, those flares were quick thinking. The invaders have been surrounded by RAF personnel. They're being rounded up

194

and taken back to RAF Mount Pleasant.' He looked back over his shoulder. 'We should get there too. If you've quite finished here,' he added with a twinkle in his eye.

He removed a radio from a pouch in his wetsuit and made a call. Two minutes later, a helicopter was setting down on the grassland nearby. They boarded and within seconds were airborne. From the air, Max could see more helicopters buzzing like flies around the invasion beach. He looked out across the South Atlantic. It was still stormy and threatening. He shivered at the memory of what they had all gone through, then turned away. He'd seen quite enough of the ocean for the time being.

The helicopter landed at the RAF base. Stepping out of the chopper, the cadets immediately saw the results of their night's work. Argentine soldiers were being led into an aircraft hangar at gunpoint, their heads down, their body language deflated. More helicopters were flying in and out, delivering prisoners of war and returning to collect more. British army and RAF personnel were shouting instructions across the airfield. Military trucks swarmed everywhere. The whole place seemed to throb anxiously.

There were civilians here too, being delivered to the safety of the base by truck. Max assumed that they were being temporarily evacuated from Port Stanley. As he and Abby followed Woody to what seemed to be a deserted hangar, a voice shouted his name.

'Max! *Max!*'

He turned in astonishment and saw a boy running towards him. It took him a moment to realise who it was: Marcus, the kid from the whale-watching trip. By that time, Marcus was standing breathlessly in front of him.

'Have you heard?' he gabbled. 'Have you heard what happened? They came and pulled us out of bed, and there were these soldiers, and . . .'

His voice trailed off and he suddenly seemed to see Max with new eyes. Max immediately felt self-conscious. He touched his face. He guessed he was pretty messed up. His clothes were damp and filthy.

'I guess you're not looking your best,' Abby said quietly.

Marcus's mum had run after him. When she reached them, she put one arm protectively around her son's shoulders. She too looked Max up and down, but with an expression Max couldn't quite work out. Was it disapproval? Was it fear? Whatever it was, she clearly didn't want her son anywhere near him. She hustled him away to where the other civilians were congregating. Marcus looked back over his shoulder, slightly awed, slightly scared. He didn't seem sad that his mother was moving him on.

'Get used to it, buddy,' Woody said. 'It can be a lonely business, saving people's lives.'

'Yeah, well,' Max said, 'if I wanted to be famous, I'd go on *Britain's Got Talent*.'

'Me too,' Abby said. 'You reckon you'd get a golden buzzer for hijacking an enemy ship?'

Max didn't answer. Something else had caught his eye. Across the airstrip, an older woman was being led away by two soldiers. It was Arlene from the guest house. She looked over in their direction. Her expression was flat and unfriendly.

'Forgot to tell you,' Abby said. 'I think Arlene had more on her plate than sausages.' When Max raised an eyebrow, she added: 'I think she was informing on us.'

They found the others waiting for them in the hangar, along with Angel. In one corner was a wall-mounted TV. It was on mute, but showed breaking news of military activity in the Falklands. Of course, it didn't mention the cadets. Max had never seen his friends more exhausted or bedraggled. Lukas was limping. He, Sami and Lili looked nauseous. Max could tell something bad had happened. Lukas especially wore a haunted expression. Max walked up to him and put one hand on his shoulder. 'You okay?' he asked.

Lukas nodded silently, then averted his eyes.

'What is it?' Max asked.

'Our friend with the red eyes,' Lukas said. 'Put it this way, turns out he was heavier than a skua. He was going to kill us. We tricked him into the minefield, but I didn't mean for him to . . .' He trailed off.

Max was silent. He was aware of all the others watching them silently.

'It was a bad way to go,' Lukas said finally. '*Really* bad.'

Lili stepped forward. 'It was us or him,' she said. 'He'd already killed the farmer. He'd have killed the three of us like that.' She snapped her fingers.

'Then it's not just the lives of the Falkland islanders you've saved tonight,' Max said. 'It's the lives of your friends too.'

Woody and Angel approached them. 'In battle,' Angel said, 'people die. But sometimes more people would die without the battle. I think that might have been the case tonight, if it weren't for you five.'

'Maybe I'm just not cut out for watching people being blown to bits,' Lukas said bitterly.

'I'd be worried if you were,' Angel replied. She put her arms around Lukas and hugged him. To Max's slight surprise, Lukas didn't resist. 'There's going to be a lot of talk around the world about what happened today,' she said, glancing up towards the rolling news on the TV. 'You lot won't be mentioned in any of it. No thank-yous, no glory. That's life in the special forces. I hope you're comfortable with that?'

The cadets looked at each other, their faces deadly serious, and nodded.

'Good. Then let's get you out of here.'

'Are you saying our holiday's over?' Abby asked.

'Yeah,' Angel said. 'Holiday's over. It's time to go home.'

Look out for more from the

SPECIAL FORCES CADETS

Chris Ryan

Chris Ryan was born in Newcastle.

In 1984 he joined 22 SAS. After completing the year-long Alpine Guides Course, he was the troop guide for B Squadron Mountain Troop. He completed three tours with the anti-terrorist team, serving as an assaulter, sniper and finally Sniper Team Commander.

Chris was part of the SAS eight-man patrol chosen for the famous Bravo Two Zero mission during the 1991 Gulf War. He was the only member of the unit to escape from Iraq, where three of his colleagues were killed and four captured. This was the longest escape and evasion in the history of the SAS, and for this he was awarded the Military Medal. Chris wrote about his experiences in his book *The One That Got Away*, which was adapted for screen and became an immediate bestseller.

Since then he has written five other books of non-fiction, over twenty bestselling novels and three series of children's books. Chris's novels have gone on to inspire the Sky One series *Strike Back*.

In addition to his books, Chris has presented a number of very successful TV programmes including *Hunting Chris Ryan*, *How Not to Die* and *Chris Ryan's Elite Police*.

Thank you for choosing a Hot Key book.

If you want to know more about our authors and what we publish, you can find us online.

You can start at our website

www.hotkeybooks.com

And you can also find us on:

We hope to see you soon!